Nora Roberts is the *New York Times* bestselling author of more than one hundred and ninety novels. A born storyteller, she creates a blend of warmth, humour and poignancy that speaks directly to her readers and has earned her almost every award for excellence in her field. The youngest of five children, Nora Roberts lives in western Maryland. She has two sons.

Visit her website at www.noraroberts.com.

Nora Roberts

Nightshade

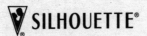

Published in Great Britain 2009. This edition 2011.
Silhouette Books, an imprint of Harlequin (UK) Limited,
Eton House, 18-24 Paradise Road, Richmond, Surrey TW9 1SR

© Nora Roberts 1993

ISBN: 978 0 263 89009 9

026-0511

Harlequin (UK) policy is to use papers that are natural, renewable
and recyclable products and made from wood grown in sustainable
forests. The logging and manufacturing processes conform to the legal
environmental regulations of the country of origin.

Printed and bound by
CPI Group (UK) Ltd, Croydon, CR0 4YY

For Dan

Prologue

It was a hell of a place to meet a snitch. A cold night, a dark street, with the smell of whiskey and sweat seeping through the pores of the bar door at his back. Colt drew easily on a slim cigar as he studied the spindly bag of bones who'd agreed to sell him information. Not much to look at, Colt mused—short, skinny, and ugly as homemade sin. In the garish light tossed fitfully by the neon sign behind them, his informant looked almost comical.

But there was nothing funny about the business at hand.

"You're a hard man to pin down, Billings."

"Yeah, yeah…" Billings nibbled on a grimy thumb, his gaze sweeping up and down the street. "A guy keeps healthy that way. Heard you were looking for me." He studied Colt, his eyes flying up, then away, soaring on nerves. "Man in my position has to be careful, you know? What you want to buy, it don't come cheap. And it's dangerous. I'd feel better with my cop. Generally I work through the cop, but I ain't been able to get through all day."

"I'd feel better without your cop. And I'm the one who's paying." To illustrate his point, Colt drew two fifties from his shirt pocket. He watched Billings's eyes dart toward the bills and linger greedily. Colt might be a man who'd take risks, but buying a pig in a poke wasn't his style. He held the money out of reach.

"Talk better if I had a drink." Billings jerked his head toward the doorway of the bar behind them. A woman's laugh, high and shrill, burst through the glass like a gunshot.

"You talk just fine to me." The man was a bundle of raw nerves, Colt observed. He could almost hear the thin bones rattle together as Billings shifted from foot to foot. If he didn't press his point now, the man was going to run like a rabbit. And he'd come too far and had too much at stake to lose him now. "Tell me what I need to know, then I'll buy you a drink."

"You're not from around here."

"No." Colt lifted a brow, waited. "Is that a problem?"

"Nope. Better you aren't. They get wind of you…" Billings swiped the back of his hand over his mouth. "Well, you look like you can handle yourself okay."

"I've been known to." He took one last drag before flicking the cigar away. Its single red eye gleamed in the gutter. "Information, Billings." To show good faith, Colt held out one of the bills. "Let's do business."

Even as Billings's eager fingers reached out, the frigid air was shattered by the shriek of tires on pavement.

Colt didn't have to read the terror in Billings's eyes. Adrenaline and instinct took over, with a kick as quick and hard as a mule's. He was diving for cover as the first shots rang out.

Chapter 1

Althea didn't mind being bored. After a rough day, a nice spot of tedium could be welcome, giving both mind and body a chance to recharge. She didn't really mind coming off a tough ten-hour shift after an even more grueling sixty-hour week and donning cocktail wear or slipping her tired feet into three-inch heels. She wouldn't even complain about being stuck at a banquet table in the ballroom of the Brown House while speech after droning speech muddled her head.

What she *did* mind was having her date's hand slide up her thigh under cover of the white linen tablecloth.

Men were so predictable.

She picked up her wineglass and, shifting in her seat, nuzzled her date's ear. "Jack?"

His fingers crept higher. "Mmm-hmm?"

"If you don't move your hand—say, within the next two seconds—I'm going to stab it, really, really hard, with my dessert fork. It would hurt, Jack." She sat back and sipped her wine, smiling over the rim as he arched a brow. "You wouldn't play racquetball for a month."

Jack Holmsby, eligible bachelor, feared prosecutor, and guest of honor at the Denver Bar Association Banquet, knew how to handle women. And he'd been trying to get close enough to handle this particular woman for months.

"Thea…" He breathed her name, gifting her with his most charming, crooked smile. "We're nearly done here. Why don't we go back to my place? We can…" He whispered into her ear a suggestion that was descriptive, inventive and possibly anatomically impossible.

Althea was saved from answering—and Jack was spared minor surgery—by the sound of her beeper. Several of her tablemates began shifting, checking pockets and purses. Inclining her head, she rose.

"Pardon me. I believe it's mine." She walked

away with a subtle switch of hips, a long flash of leg. The compact body in the backless purple dress glinting with silver beading caused more than one head to turn. Blood pressures were elevated. Fantasies were woven.

Not unaware, but certainly unconcerned, Althea strode out of the ballroom and into the lobby, toward a bank of phones. Opening her beaded evening bag, which contained a compact, lipstick, ID, emergency cash and her nine-millimeter, she fished out a quarter and made her call.

"Grayson." While she listened, she pushed back her fall of flame-colored hair. Her eyes, a tawny shade of brown, narrowed. "I'm on my way."

She hung up, turned and watched Jack Holmsby hurry toward her. An attractive man, she thought objectively. Nicely polished on the outside. A pity he was so ordinary on the inside.

"Sorry, Jack. I have to go."

Irritation scored a deep line between his brows. He had a bottle of Napoleon brandy, a stack of apple wood and a set of white satin sheets waiting at home. "Really, Thea, can't someone else take the call?"

"No." The job came first. It always came first. "It's handy I had to meet you here, Jack. You can stay and enjoy yourself."

But he wasn't giving up that easily. He dogged her through the lobby and out into the brisk fall night. "Why don't you come by after you've finished? We can pick up where we left off."

"We haven't left off, Jack." She handed her parking stub to an attendant. "You have to start to leave off, and I have no intention of starting anything with you."

She only sighed as he slipped his arms around her. "Come on, Thea, you didn't come here tonight to eat prime rib and listen to a bunch of lawyers make endless speeches." He lowered his head and murmured against her lips, "You didn't wear a dress like that to keep me at arm's length. You wore it to make me hot. And you did."

Mild irritation became brittle and keen. "I came here tonight because I respect you as a lawyer." The quick elbow to his ribs had his breath woofing out and allowed her to step back. "And because I thought we could spend a pleasant evening together. What I wear is my business, Holmsby, but I didn't choose it so that you'd grope me under the table or make ludicrous suggestions as to how I might spend the rest of my evening."

She wasn't shouting, but neither was she bothering to keep her voice down. Anger glinted in her

voice, like ice under fog. Appalled, Jack tugged at
the knot of his tie and darted glances right and
left.

"For God's sake, Althea, keep it down."

"Exactly what I was going to suggest to you,"
she said sweetly.

Though the attendant was all eyes and ears, he
politely cleared his throat. Althea turned to accept
her keys. "Thank you." She offered him a smile
and a generous tip. The smile had his heart skip-
ping a beat, and he didn't glance at the bill before
tucking it into his pocket. He was too busy dreaming.

"Ah…drive carefully, miss. And come back
soon. Real soon."

"Thanks." She tossed her hair back, then slid
gracefully behind the wheel of her reconditioned
Mustang convertible. "See you in court, Coun-
selor." Althea gunned the engine and peeled out.

Murder scenes, whether indoors or out, in an
urban, suburban or pastoral setting, had one thing in
common: the aura of death. As a cop with nearly ten
years' experience, Althea had learned to recognize
it, absorb it and file it away, while going about the
precise and mechanical business of investigation.

When Althea arrived, a half block had been secured. The police photographer had finished recording the scene and was already packing up his gear. The body had been identified. That was why she was here.

Three black-and-whites sat, their lights flashing blue and their radios coughing static. Spectators—for death always drew them—were straining against the yellow police tape, greedy, Althea knew, for a glimpse of death to reaffirm that they were alive and untouched.

Because the night was cool, she grabbed the wrap she'd tossed into the back seat of her car. The emerald-green silk kept the chill off her arms and back. Flashing her badge to the rookie handling crowd control, she slipped under the barricade. She was grateful when she spotted Sweeney, a hard-bitten cop who had twice her years on the job and was in no hurry to give up his uniform.

"Lieutenant." He nodded to her, then took out a handkerchief and made a valiant attempt to clear his stuffy nose.

"What have we got here, Sweeney?"

"Drive-by." He stuffed the handkerchief back into his pocket. "Dead guy was standing in front of the bar, talking." He gestured to the shattered window of the Tick Tock. "Witnesses say a car came by, moving north, fast. Sprayed the area with bullets and kept going."

She could still smell the blood, though it was no longer fresh. "Any bystanders hit?"

"Nope. Couple of cuts from flying glass, that's all. They hit their mark." He glanced over his shoulder, and down. "He didn't have a chance, Lieutenant. Sorry."

"Yeah, me too." She stared down at the form sprawled on the stained concrete. There'd been nothing much to him to begin with, she thought. Now there was less. He'd been five-five, maybe a hundred and ten soaking wet, spindly bones and had had a face even a mother would have been hard-pressed to love.

Wild Bill Billings, part-time pimp, part-time grifter and full-time snitch.

And, damn it, he'd been hers.

"Forensics?"

"Been and gone," Sweeney confirmed. "We're ready to put him on ice."

"Then do it. Got a list of witnesses?"

"Yeah, mostly useless. It was a black car, it was a blue car. One drunk claims it was a chariot driven by flaming demons." He swore with inventive expertise, knowing Althea well enough not to worry about her taking offense.

"We'll take what we can get." She scanned the crowd—bar types, teenagers looking for action, a scattering of the homeless and—

Her antenna vibrated as she locked in on one man. Unlike the others, he wasn't goggle-eyed with either revulsion or excitement. He stood at his ease, his leather bomber jacket open to the wind, revealing a chambray shirt, a glint of silver on a chain. His rangy build made her think he'd be fast on his feet. Snug, worn jeans rode down long legs and ended at scuffed boots. Hair that might have been dark blond or brown ruffled in the breeze and curled well over his collar.

He smoked a thin cigar, his eyes scanning the scene as hers had. The light wasn't good, but she decided he looked tanned, which suited the sharply defined face. The eyes were deep-set, and the nose was long, and just shy of being narrow. The mouth was strong, the kind that looked as though it could thin into a sneer easily.

Some instinct had her dubbing him a pro before his eyes shifted and locked on hers with an impact like a bare-fisted punch.

"Who's the cowboy, Sweeney?"

"The— Oh." Sweeney's tired face creased in what might have been a smile. Damned if she hadn't called it, he thought. The guy looked as though he should be wearing a Stetson and riding a mustang. "Witness," he told her. "Victim was talking to him when he got hit."

"Is that so?" She didn't look around when the coroner's team dealt with the body. There was no need to.

"He's the only one to give us a coherent account." Sweeney pulled out his pad, wet his thumb and flipped pages. "Says it was a black '91 Buick sedan, Colorado plates Able Charlie Frank. Says he missed the numbers 'cause the plate lights were out and he was a little busy diving for cover. Says the weapon sounded like an AK-47."

"Sounded like?" Interesting, she thought. She'd kept her eyes level with her witness's. "Maybe—" She broke off when she spotted her captain crossing the street. Captain Boyd Fletcher walked directly to the witness, shook his head, then grinned and enveloped the other man in the masculine equivalent of an embrace. There was a lot of back-thumping.

"Looks as though the captain's handling him for now." Althea pocketed her curiosity as she would a treat to be saved for later. "Let's finish up here, Sweeney."

Colt had watched her from the moment one long, smooth leg swung out of the door of the Mustang. A lady like that was worth watching—well worth it. He'd liked the way she moved—with an athletic and economical grace that wasted neither time nor energy. Certainly he'd liked the way she looked. Her neat, sexy little body had just enough curves to whet a man's appetite, and with all that green-and-purple silk rippling in the wind... The sunburst of hair, blowing away from a cool cameo face, brought much more interesting things to a man's mind than his grandmother's heirloom jewelry.

It was a cold night, and one look at that well-packed number had Colt thinking about heat.

It wasn't such a bad way to keep warm while he waited. He wasn't a man who waited well under the best of circumstances.

He hadn't been particularly surprised to see her flash ID to the baby-faced cop at the barricade. She carried authority beautifully on her luscious swimmer's shoulders. Idly lighting a cigar, he decided she was an assistant D.A., then realized his error when she went into conference with Sweeney.

The lady had *cop* written all over her.

Late twenties, he figured, maybe five-four without those ankle-wrecking heels, and a tidy one-ten.

They sure were making cops in interesting packages these days.

So he waited, sizing up the scene. He didn't have any feelings one way or the other about the remains of Wild Bill Billings. The man was no good to him now.

He'd dig up something, or someone, else. Colt Nightshade wasn't a man to let murder get in his way.

When he felt her watching him, he drew smoke in lazily, chuffed it out. Then he shifted his gaze until it met hers. The tightening in his gut was unexpected—it was raw and purely sexual. The one fleeting instant when his mind was wiped clean as glass was more than unexpected. It was unprecedented. Power slapped against power. She took a step toward him. He let out the breath he'd just realized he was holding.

His preoccupation made it easy for Boyd to come up behind him and catch him unawares.

"Colt! Son of a bitch!"

Colt turned, braced and ready for anything. But the flat intensity in his eyes faded into a grin that might have melted any woman within twenty paces.

"Fletch." With the easy warmth he reserved for friends, Colt returned the bear hug before stepping back to take stock. He hadn't seen Boyd in nearly ten years. It relieved him to see that so little had changed. "Still got that pretty face, don't you?"

"And you still sound like you've just ridden in off the range. God, it's good to see you. When'd you get into town?"

"Couple of days ago. I wanted to take care of some business before I got in touch."

Boyd looked past him to where the coroner's van was being loaded. "Was that your business?"

"Part of it. I appreciate you coming down like this."

"Yeah." Boyd spotted Althea, acknowledging her with an imperceptible nod. "Did you call a cop, Colt, or a friend?"

Colt looked down at the stub of his cigar, dropped it near the gutter and crushed it with his boot. "It's handy, you being both."

"Did you kill that guy?"

It was asked so matter-of-factly, that Colt grinned again. He knew Boyd wouldn't have turned a hair if he'd confessed then and there. "Nope."

Boyd nodded again. "Going to fill me in?"

"Yep."

"Why don't you wait in the car? I'll be with you in a minute."

"*Captain* Boyd Fletcher." Colt shook his head and chuckled. Though it was after midnight, he was as alert as he was relaxed, a cup of bad coffee in his hand and his scruffy boots propped on Boyd's desk. "Ain't that just something?"

"I thought you were raising horses and cattle in Wyoming."

"I do." His voice was a drawl, with the faintest whisper of a twang. "Now and again I do."

"What happened to the law degree?"

"Oh, it's around somewhere."

"And the air force?"

"I still fly. Just don't wear a uniform anymore. How long's it going to take for that pizza to get here?"

"Just long enough for it to be cold and inedible." Boyd leaned back in his chair. He was comfortable in his office. He was comfortable on the street. And, as he had been twenty years ago, in their prep school days, he was comfortable with Colt.

"You didn't get a look at the shooter?"

"Hell, Fletch, I was lucky to make the car before I was diving for cover and chewing asphalt. Not that that's going to help much. Odds are it was stolen."

"Lieutenant Grayson's tracking it. Now, why don't you tell me what you were doing with Wild Bill?"

"He contacted me. I've bee—" He broke off when Althea strolled in. She hadn't bothered to knock, and she was carrying a flat cardboard box.

"You two order pizza?" She dropped the box onto Boyd's desk, held out a hand. "Ten bucks, Fletcher."

"Althea Grayson, Colt Nightshade. Colt's an old friend." Boyd dug ten dollars out of his wallet. After folding the bill neatly and tucking it in a pocket of her purse, she set her beaded bag on a stack of files.

"Mr. Nightshade."

"Ms. Grayson."

"*Lieutenant* Grayson," she corrected. Popping up the lid on the box, she perused the contents, chose a slice. "I believe you were at my crime scene."

"Sure did look that way." He lowered his legs so that he could lean forward and take a piece himself. He caught her scent over the aroma of cooling sausage pizza. It was a whole lot more tantalizing.

"Thanks," she murmured when Boyd passed her a napkin. "I wondered what you were doing there, getting shot at with my snitch."

Colt's eyes narrowed. "Your snitch?"

"That's right." Like his hair, his eyes couldn't seem to decide what color they should be, Althea thought. They were caught somewhere between blue and green. And at the moment they were as cold as the wind whipping at the window.

"Bill told me he tried to reach his police contact off and on all day."

"I was in the field."

Colt's brow arched as he skimmed his gaze over the swirl of emerald silk. "Some field."

"Lieutenant Grayson spent all day putting the cap on a drug operation," Boyd interjected. "Now, kids, why don't we start over, and at the beginning?"

"Fine." Setting her half-eaten slice down, Althea wiped her fingers, then removed her wrap. Colt clenched his teeth to keep his tongue from falling out. Because she was turned away from him, Colt had the painful pleasure of gauging just how allur-

ing a naked back could be when it was slim,
straight and framed in purple silk.

After laying her coat over a file cabinet, Althea
reclaimed her pizza and sat on the corner of
Boyd's desk.

She knew just what she did to a man, Colt realized. He could see that smug, faintly amused female knowledge in her eyes. Colt had always
figured every woman knew her own arsenal down
to the last eyelash, but it was tough on a man when
the woman was as heavily armed as this.

"Wild Bill, Mr. Nightshade…" Althea began.
"What were you doing with him?"

"Talking." He knew his answer was obstinate,
but at the moment he was trying to judge whether
there was anything between the sexy lieutenant
and his old friend. His old *married* friend, Colt
mused. He was relieved, and more than a little surprised not to scent even a whiff of attraction between them.

"About?" Althea's voice was still patient, even
pleasant. As if, Colt thought, she were questioning a small boy who was mentally deficient.

"The victim was Thea's snitch," Boyd reminded
Colt. "If she wants the case—"

"And I do."

"Then it's hers."

To buy himself time, Colt reached for another slice of pizza. He was going to have to do something he hated, something that stuck in his craw like bad beef jerky. He was going to have to ask for help. And to get it he was going to have to share what he knew.

"It took me two days to track down Billings and get him to agree to talk to me." It had also cost him two hundred in bribes to clear the path, but he wasn't one to count the cost until the final tally. "He was nervous, didn't really want to talk unless he had his police contact with him. So I made it worth his while."

He glanced back at Althea. The lady was wiped out, he realized. The fatigue was hard to spot, but it was there—in the slight drooping of her eyelids, the faint shadows under them.

"I'm sorry you lost him, but I don't think your being there would have changed anything."

"We won't know that, will we?" She wouldn't let the regret color her voice, or her judgment. "Why did you go to so much trouble to contact Bill?"

"He used to have a girl working for him. Jade. Probably her street name."

Althea let her mind click back, nodded. "Yeah. Little blonde, baby face. She took a couple of busts for solicitation. I'll have to check, but I don't think she's worked the stroll for four or five weeks."

"That'd be about right." Colt rose to fill his cup with more of the sludge from the automatic brewer. "It would have been about that long ago that Billings got her a job. In the movies." If he was going to drink poison, he'd take it like a man, without any cream or sugar to cut the bite. Sipping, he turned back. "I ain't talking Hollywood. This was the down-and-dirty stuff, for private viewers who have the taste and the money to buy thrills. Videotapes for hard-core connoisseurs." He shrugged and sat again. "Can't say it bothers me any, if we're talking about consenting adults. Though I prefer my sex in the flesh."

"But we're not talking about you, Mr. Nightshade."

"Oh, you don't have to call me *mister*, Lieutenant. Seems cold, when we're discussing such warm topics." Smiling, he leaned back. He had yet to ruffle her feathers, and for reasons he wasn't going to take the time to explore, he wanted to ruffle them good and proper. "Well, as it happens, something spooked Jade and she lit out. I'm not one to think a hooker's got a heart of gold, but this one at least had a conscience. She sent off a letter to a Mr. and Mrs. Frank Cook." He shifted his gaze to Boyd. "Frank and Marleen Cook."

"Marleen?" Boyd's brows shot up. "Marleen and Frank?"

"The same." Colt's smile was wry. "More old friends, Lieutenant. As it happens, I was what you might call intimate friends with Mrs. Cook about a million years ago. Being a woman of sound judgment, she married Frank, settled down in Albuquerque and had herself a couple of beautiful kids."

Althea shifted, crossed her legs with a rustle of silk. The silver dangling over his shirt was a Saint Christopher medal, she noted. The patron saint of travelers. She wondered if Mr. Nightshade felt the need for spiritual protection.

"I assume this is leading somewhere other than down memory lane?"

"Oh, it's leading right back to your professional front door, Lieutenant. I just prefer the circular route now and then." He took out a cigar, running it through his long fingers before reaching for his lighter. "About a month ago, Marleen's oldest girl—that's Elizabeth. You ever meet Liz, Boyd?"

Boyd shook his head. He didn't like where this was heading. Not one bit. "Not since she was in diapers. What is she, twelve?"

"Thirteen. Just." Colt flicked his lighter on, sucked his cigar to life. Thought he knew, all too well, that the tang of smoke wouldn't cloud the bitter taste in his throat. "Pretty as a picture, like her mama. Got Marleen's hair-trigger temper, too. There was some trouble at home, the kind I imagine most families have some time or other. But Liz got her back up and took off."

"She ran away?" Althea understood the runaway's mind well. Too well.

"Tossed a few things in her backpack and took off. Needless to say, Marleen and Frank have been living in hell the past few weeks. They contacted the police, but the official route wasn't getting them very far." He blew out smoke. "No offense. Ten days ago they called me."

"Why?" Althea asked.

"Told you. We're friends."

"Do you usually track down pimps and dodge bullets for friends?"

She had a way with sarcasm, all right, Colt mused. It was one more weapon in the arsenal. "I do favors for people."

"Are you a licensed investigator?"

Pursing his lips, Colt studied the tip of his cigar. "I'm not big on licenses. I put out some feelers, had a little luck tracing her north. Then the Cooks got Jade's letter." Clamping his cigar between his teeth, he drew a folded sheet of floral stationery from his inside jacket pocket. "Save time if you read it yourself," he said, and passed it to Boyd. Althea rose, going behind Boyd's back, laying a hand on his shoulder as she read with him.

It was a curiously intimate and yet asexual gesture. One, Colt decided, that spoke of friendship and trust.

The handwriting was as girlishly fussy as the paper. But the content, Althea noted, had nothing to do with flowers and ribbons and childhood fancies.

Dear Mr. and Mrs. Cook,
I met Liz in Denver. She is a nice kid. I know she is really sorry she ran away and would come back now if she could. I would help her out, but I got to get out of town. Liz is in trouble. I would go to the cops, but I'm scared and I don't think they listen to someone like me. She is not cut out for the life, but they won't

let her go. She is young and so pretty, and they are making lots of money from the movies I think. I have been in the life for five years, but some of the stuff they want us to do for the camera gives me the creeps. I think they killed one of the girls, so I am getting out before they kill me. Liz gave me your address and asked me to write and say she was sorry. She's real scared and I hope you find her okay.

Jade

P.S. They have a place up in the mountains where they do the movies. And there is an apartment on Second Avenue.

Boyd didn't give the letter back, but laid it on his desk. He had a daughter of his own. He thought of Allison, sweet, feisty and six, and had to swallow a hot ball of sick rage.

"You could have come to me with this. You *should* have come to me."

"I'm used to working alone." Colt drew on his cigar again before tamping it out. "In any case, I intended to come to you after I put a few things together. I got the name of Jade's pimp, and I wanted to shake him down."

"And now he's dead." Althea's voice was flat as she turned to stare out of Boyd's window.

"Yeah." Colt studied her profile. It wasn't just anger he felt from her. There was a lot more mixed up with it. "Word must have gotten back that I was looking for him, and that he was willing to talk to me. Leads me to think that we're dealing with well-connected slime, and slime that doesn't blink at murder."

"This is a police matter, Colt," Boyd said quietly.

"No argument." Ready to deal, he spread his hands. "It's also a personal matter. I'm going to keep digging, Fletch. There's no law against it. I'm the Cooks' representative—their lawyer, if we need a handle."

"Is that what you are?" Her emotions under control again, Althea turned back to him. "A lawyer?"

"When it suits me. I don't want to interfere with your investigation," he said to Boyd. "I want the kid back—safely back—with Marleen and Frank. I'll cooperate completely. Anything I know, you'll know. But it has to be quid pro quo. Give me a cop to work with on this, Boyd." He smiled a little— just a quirk at the corner of his mouth, as if he were amused at himself. "And you of all people know how much I hate asking for an official partner on a job. But it's Liz that matters, all that matters. You know I'm good." He leaned forward. "You know I won't back off. Let me have your best man, and let's get these bastards."

Boyd pressed his fingers to his tired eyes. He could, of course, order Colt to back off. And he'd be wasting his breath. He could refuse to cooperate, could refuse to share any information the department unearthed. And Colt would work around him. Yes, he knew Colt was good, and he had some idea of the kind of work he'd done while in the military.

It would hardly be the first time Boyd Fletcher had bent the rules. His decision made, he gestured toward Althea.

"She's my best man."

Chapter 2

If a man had to have a partner, she might as well
be easy on the eyes. In any case, Colt didn't intend
to work *with* Althea so much as *through* her. She
would be his conduit to the official end of the investigation. He'd keep his word—he always did,
except when he didn't—and feed her whatever information he gleaned. Not that he expected her to
do much with it.

There were only a handful of cops Colt respected, with Boyd topping the list. As far as Lieutenant Grayson was concerned, Colt figured she'd
be decorative, marginally helpful and little else.

The badge, the bod and the sarcasm would probably be useful when it came to interviewing any possible connections.

At least he'd had a decent night's sleep—all six hours of it. He hadn't protested when Boyd insisted he check out of his hotel and check into the Fletcher household for the duration of his stay. Colt liked families—other people's, in any case—and he'd been curious about Boyd's wife.

He'd missed their wedding. Though he wasn't particularly fond of the spit and polish ceremonies called for, he would have gone. But it was a long way from Beirut to Denver, and he'd been busy with terrorists at the time.

He was delighted with Cilla. The woman hadn't turned a hair at having her husband bring home a strange man at 2:00 a.m. Bundled in a terry-cloth robe, she'd offered him the guest room, with the suggestion that if he wanted to sleep in he should put the pillow over his head. The kids apparently rose at seven to get ready for school.

He'd slept like a rock, and when he'd awakened to the sounds of shouts and clomping feet, he'd taken his hostess's advice and had caught another hour of sleep with his head buried.

Now, fortified by an excellent breakfast and

three cups of first-class coffee prepared by the Fletchers' housekeeper, he was ready to roll.

His agreement with Boyd made the precinct house his first stop. He'd check in with Althea, grill her on any associates of Billings's, then go his own way.

It seemed to him that his old friend ran a tight ship. There was the usual din of ringing phones, clattering keyboards and raised voices inside the station. There were the usual scents of coffee, industrial-strength cleaners and sweaty bodies. But there was also an underlying sense of organization and purpose.

The desk sergeant had Colt's name, and he handed him a visitor's badge and directed him to Althea's office. Past the bull pen, and two doors down a narrow corridor he found her door. It was shut, so he rapped once before pushing it open. He knew she was there before he saw her. He scented her, as a wolf scents his mate. Or his prey.

Gone were the bold silks, but she still looked more the fashion plate than the cop. The tailored slacks and jacket in smoke gray did nothing to suggest masculinity. Nor did he think she chose to deny her sex, for she'd accented the suit with a soft pink blouse and a star-shaped jeweled lapel pin.

Her mass of hair had been trained back in some complicated braid that left her face softly framed. Two heavy twists of gold glinted at her ears.

The result was as neat as any maiden aunt could want, and still had the knockout punch of frosted sex.

A lesser man might have licked his lips.

"Grayson."

"Nightshade." She gestured toward a chair. "Have a seat."

There was only one to spare, straight-backed and wood. Colt turned it around and straddled it. As he did, he noted that her office was less than half the size of Boyd's, and ruthlessly organized. File drawers were neatly closed, papers properly stacked, pencils sharpened to lethal points. There was a plant on one of the rear corners of the desk that he was sure was meticulously watered. There were no pictures of family or friends. The only spot of color in the small, windowless room was a painting, an abstract in vivid blues, greens and reds. Slashes of colors that clashed and warred, rather than melded.

Some instinct told him it suited her down to the ground.

"So." He folded his arms over the back of the

chair and leaned forward. "You run the shooter's car through Motor Vehicles?"

"Didn't have to. It was on this morning's hot sheet." She took her copy and offered it. "Reported stolen at eleven o'clock last night. Owners had been out for dinner, came out of the restaurant and found the car gone. Dr. and Dr. Wilmer, a couple of dentists celebrating their fifth anniversary. Looks like they're clean."

"Probably." He tossed the sheet back onto her desk. He hadn't really believed he'd find a connection through the car. "Don't guess it's turned up?"

"Not yet. I've got Jade's rap sheet, if you're interested." After replacing the hot sheet in its proper place, she picked up a file. "Janice Willowby. Age twenty-two. Couple of busts for solicitation—a few charges as a juvie for more of the same. One possession arrest, also as a juvenile, when she got rousted with a couple of joints in her purse. Went through the social services route, a halfway house, counseling, then turned twenty-one and went back on the streets."

It wasn't a new story. "Have we got any family? She might head home."

"A mother in Kansas City—or she was in Kansas City as of eighteen months ago. I'm trying to track her down."

"You've been busy."

"Not all of us start our day at—" she looked down at her watch "—ten."

"I do better at night, Lieutenant." He took out a cigar.

Althea eyed it, shook her head. "Not in here, pal."

Agreeably Colt tapped the cigar back into his pocket. "Who did Billings trust, other than you?"

"I don't know that he trusted anybody." But it hurt, because she knew he had trusted somebody. He'd trusted her, and somehow she'd missed a step. And now he was dead. "We had an arrangement. I gave him money, he gave me information."

"What kind?"

"With Wild Bill, it came in a variety pack. He had his fingers in a lot of pies. Little pies, mostly." She shifted some papers on her desk, tapping the edges neatly together. "He was strictly small-time, but he had big ears, knew how to fade into the background so you forgot he was around. People talked around him, because he looked like his brain would fit in a teacup. But he was smart." Her voice changed, tipping Colt off to something she had yet to admit even to herself. She was grieving. "Smart enough to keep from crossing the line that would send him up to hard time. Smart enough to keep from stepping on the wrong toes. Until last night."

"I didn't make any secret of the fact I was looking for him, and for information he could give me. But I sure as hell didn't want him dead."

"I'm not blaming you."

"No?"

"No." She pushed away from the desk far enough to allow her to swivel the chair around and face him. "People like Bill, no matter how smart, have short life expectancies. If he'd have been able to contact me, I might have met him at the same spot you did, with the same results." She'd thought that through, carefully, ruthlessly. "I might not like your style, Nightshade, but I'm not pinning this on you."

She sat very still, he noted, no gestures, no shrugs, no restless tapping. Like the painting on the wall behind her, she communicated vibrant passion without movement.

"And just what is my style, Lieutenant?"

"You're a renegade. The kind who doesn't just refuse to play by the rules, but rejoices in breaking them." Her eyes stayed level with his, and were cool as lake water. He wondered what it would take to warm them up. "You start things, but you don't always finish them. Maybe that means you bore easily, or you just run out of energy. Either way, it doesn't say much about your dependability."

Her rundown of his personality annoyed him, but when he spoke again, his slow southwestern drawl was amused. "You figured all that out since last night?"

"I ran a make on you. The prep school where you hung out with Boyd surprised me." Her lips curved, but the eyes had yet to warm. "You don't look like the preppie type."

"My parents thought it would tame me." He grinned. "Guess not."

"Neither did Harvard, where you got your law degree—which you haven't put to much use. Parts of your military career were classified, but all in all, I got the picture." There was a dish of sugared almonds on her desk. Althea leaned over and, after careful deliberation, chose the one she wanted. "I don't work with someone I don't know."

"Me either. So why don't you fill me in on Althea Grayson?"

"I'm the cop," she said simply. "And you're not. I assume you have a recent picture of Elizabeth Cook?"

"Yeah, I got one." But he didn't reach for it. He

didn't have to take this kind of bull from some glamourpuss with a badge. "Tell me, Lieutenant, just who jammed a stick up your—"

The phone cut him off, which, considering the flash in Althea's eye, might have been for the best. At least he knew how to defrost those eyes now.

"Grayson." She waited a beat, then jotted something down on a pad. "Notify Forensics. I'm on my way." She rose, tucking the pad into a snakeskin purse. "We found the car." She was frowning when she slung the bag over her shoulder. "Since Boyd wants you in, you can come along for the ride—as an observer only. Got it?"

"Oh, yeah. I got it fine."

He followed her out, then quickly moved up so that they walked side by side. The woman had the best rear view this side of the Mississippi, and Colt didn't care to be distracted.

"I didn't have much time to play catch-up with Boyd last night," he began. "I wondered how it was that you're on such…easy terms with your captain."

She was walking down the stairs to the garage, and she stopped, turned, aimed one razor-sharp glance.

"What?" he demanded as she assessed him silently.

"I'm trying to decide if you're insulting me and

Boyd—in which case I'd have to hurt you—or if you simply phrased your question badly."

He lifted a brow. "Try the second choice."

"All right." She continued down. "We were partners for over seven years." She reached the bottom of the steps and turned sharply to the right. The flat heels of her suede half boots clicked busily on the concrete. "When you trust someone with your life on a day-to-day basis, you'd better be on easy terms."

"Then he made captain."

"That's right." After taking out her keys, she unlocked her car. "Sorry, but the passenger seat's stuck all the way forward. I haven't had time to take it in and get it fixed."

Colt looked down at the spiffy sports car with some regret. A sexy car, sure, but with the seat in that position, he was going to have to fold himself up like an accordion and sit with his chin on his knees. "And you don't have a problem with that— Boyd's being captain?"

Althea slid in gracefully, smirking a bit as Colt grunted and arranged himself beside her. "No. Am I ambitious? Yes. Do I resent having the best cop I ever worked with as my superior? No. Do I expect to make captain myself within another five

years? You bet your butt." She pushed mirrored
aviator sunglasses over her eyes. "Fasten your seat
belt, Nightshade." With that, she peeled out, shooting up the ramp of the garage and out onto the
street.

He had to admire her driving. He had no choice,
since she was behind the wheel and his life was in
her hands. Easy terms? he wondered. Yeah, right.
"So, you and Boyd are friends."

"That's right. Why?"

"I just wanted to establish that it wasn't all
good-looking men of a certain age who put your
back up." He grinned at her as she downshifted
around a corner. "I like knowing it's just me.
Makes me feel kind of special, you know?"

She smiled then and shot him what could have
been a friendly look. It certainly was no more than
friendly, and it really shouldn't have had his heart
doing a slow roll in his chest. "I wouldn't say you
put my back up, Nightshade. I just don't trust hot-
doggers. But since we're both after the same thing
here, and since Boyd's a pal on both sides, we can
try to get along."

"Sounds reasonable. We've got the job and
Boyd in common. Maybe we can find a couple of
other things." Her radio was turned down low. Colt

flicked the volume up and nodded approval at the slow, pulse-pumping blues. "There, that's one more thing. How do you feel about Mexican food?"

"I like my chili hot and my margaritas cold."

"Progress." He tried to shift in his seat, rapped his knee on the dash, and swore. "If we're going to do any more driving together, we take my four-wheel."

"We'll discuss it." She turned the music down again when she heard the police radio squawk to life.

"All units in the vicinity of Sheridan and Jewell, 511 in progress."

Althea swore as the dispatcher continued to call for assistance. "That's only a block down." She turned left and aimed a quick, dubious look at Colt. "Shots fired," she told him. "Police business, got it?"

"Sure."

"This is unit six responding," she said into the transmitter. "I'm on the scene." After squealing to a halt behind the black-and-white, she shoved open her door. "Stay in the car." With that terse order, she drew her weapon and headed for the entrance of a four-story apartment building.

She paused at the door, sucking in her breath. The minute she bolted through, she heard the blast of another gunshot.

One floor up, she thought. Maybe two. With her body braced and flattened against the wall, she scanned the cramped, deserted entryway, then started up. Screaming— No, she thought, crying. A child. Her mind cold, her hands steady, she swung her weapon toward the first landing, then followed it. A door opened to her left. Crouching, she aimed toward the movement and stared into the face of an elderly woman with terrified eyes.

"Police," Althea told her. "Stay inside."

The door shut. A bolt turned. Althea shifted toward the second staircase. She saw them then, the cop who was down, and the cop who was huddled over him.

"Officer." There was the snap of authority in her voice when she dropped a hand on the uninjured cop's shoulder. "What's the status here?"

"He shot Jim. He came running out with the kid and opened up."

The uniformed cop was sheet-white, she noted, as pale as his partner, who was bleeding on the stairway. She couldn't tell which of them was shaking more violently. "What's your name?"

"Harrison. Don Harrison." He was pressing a soaked handkerchief to the gaping wound low on his partner's left shoulder.

"Officer Harrison, I'm Lieutenant Grayson. Give me the situation here, and make it fast."

"Sir." He took two short, quick breaths. "Domestic dispute. Shots fired. A white male assaulted the woman in apartment 2-D. He opened fire on us and headed upstairs with a small female child as a shield."

As he finished, a woman stumbled out of the apartment above. Where she clutched her side, blood trickled through her fingers. "He took my baby. Charlie took my baby. Please, God…" She fell weeping to her knees. "He's crazy. Please, God…"

"Officer Harrison." A sound on the stairs had Althea moving fast, then swearing. She should have known Colt wouldn't stay in the car. "Get on the horn, now," she continued. "Call for backup. Officer and civilian down. Hostage situation. Now tell me what he was carrying."

"Looked like a .45."

"Make the call, then get in here and back me up." She spared one look at Colt. "Make yourself useful. Do what you can for these two."

She raced up the stairs. She could hear the baby crying again, long terrified wails that echoed in the narrow corridors. By the time she reached the top floor, she heard the slam of a door. The roof, she decided. Braced on one side of the door, she turned the knob, kicked it open and went in low.

He fired once, wildly. The bullet sang more than a foot to her right. Althea took her stand, and faced him.

"Police!" she shouted. "Put down your weapon!"

He stood near the edge of the roof, a big man. Linebacker-size, she noted, his skin flushed with rage, his eyes glazed by chemicals. That she could handle. It was a .45 he was carrying. She could handle that, as well. But it was the child, the little girl of perhaps two that he was holding by one foot over the edge of the roof, that she wasn't sure she could deal with.

"I'll drop her!" He shouted it, like a chant against the brisk wind. "I'll do it! I'll do it! I swear to God, I'll drop her like a stone!" He shook the child, who continued to scream. One of her little pink tennis shoes flew off and fell five long stories.

"You don't want to make a mistake, do you, Charlie?" Althea inched away from the door, side-stepping slowly, her nine-millimeter aimed at the broad chest. "Bring her back from the edge."

"I'm going to drop the little bitch." He grinned when he said it, his teeth bared, his eyes glittering. "She's just like her mother. Whining and crying all the damn time. Thought they could get away from me. I found them, didn't I? Linda's real sorry now, isn't she? Real damn sorry now."

"Yes, she is." She had to get to the kid. There had to be a way to get to the child. Unbidden an old, obscene memory flashed through her head. The shouting, the threats, the fear. Althea tramped on them as she would a roach. "You hurt the little girl and it's all over, Charlie."

"Don't tell me it's over!" Enraged, he swung the child like a sack of laundry. Althea's heart stopped, and so did the screaming. The little girl was merely sobbing now, quietly, helplessly, her arms dangling limply, her huge blue eyes fixed and glazed. "She tried to tell me it was over. It's over, Charlie," he mimicked in a singsong voice. "So I knocked her around some. God knows she deserved it, nagging me about getting work, nagging about every damn thing. And as soon as the kid came along, everything changed. I got no use for bitches in my life. But *I* say when it's over."

The wail of sirens rose up in the air. Althea sensed movement behind her, but didn't turn. Didn't dare. She needed the man focused on her, only on her. "Bring the kid in and you might get away. You want to get away, don't you, Charlie? Come on. Give her to me. You don't need her."

"You think I'm stupid?" His lips curled into a snarl. "You're just one more bitch."

"I don't think you're stupid." She caught a movement out of the corner of her eye, and would have sworn if she'd dared. It wasn't Harrison. It was Colt, slipping like a shadow toward the man's blind side. "I don't think you'd be stupid enough to hurt the kid." She was closer now, five feet away. Althea knew that it might as well be fifty.

"I'm going to kill her!" he shouted. "And I'm going to kill you, and I'm going to kill anybody who gets in my way! Nobody says it's over till I say it's over!"

It happened then, fast, like a blur at the corner of a dream. Colt lunged, wrapping one arm around the child's waist. Althea caught the flash of metal in his hand and recognized it as a .32. He might have used it, if saving the child hadn't been his priority. He pivoted back, swinging the child so that his body was her shield, and by the time he'd brought his weapon to bear, it was over.

Althea watched the .45 arch from her toward Colt and the girl. And she fired. The bullet drove him back. His knees hit the low curbing at the edge of the roof. He was the one who dropped like a stone.

Althea didn't permit herself even a sigh. She holstered her weapon and strode to where Colt was cuddling the weeping child. "She okay?"

"Looks like." In a move so natural she would have sworn he'd spent his life doing it, he settled the girl on his hip and kissed her damp temple. "You're okay now, baby. Nobody's going to hurt you."

"Mama." Choking on tears, she buried her face in Colt's shoulder. "Mama."

"We'll take you to your mama, honey, don't you worry." Colt still held his gun, but his other hand was busy stroking the girl's wispy blond hair. "Nice work, Lieutenant."

Althea glanced over her shoulder. Cops were already pounding up the stairs. "I've done better."

"You kept him talking so the kid had a shot, then you took him down. It doesn't get better than that." And there had been a look in her eyes, from the moment she'd started up the steps with a cop's blood on her hands. And it hadn't faded yet. A look he'd seen before, Colt mused. One he'd always termed a warrior's look.

Her eyes held his for another minute. "Let's get her out of here" was all she said.

"Fine." They started toward the door.

"Just one thing, Nightshade."

He smiled a little, certain this was the moment she'd thank him. "What's that?"

"Have you got a permit for that gun?"

He stopped, stared. Then his smile exploded into a deep, rich laugh. Charmed, the little girl looked up, sniffled, and managed a watery smile.

She didn't think about killing. Didn't permit herself. She'd killed before, and knew she would likely do so again. But she didn't think about it. She knew that if she reflected too deeply on that aspect of the job, she could freeze, or she could drink or she could grow callous. Or, worse—infinitely worse—she could grow to enjoy it.

So she filed her report and put it out of her mind. Or tried to.

She hand-carried a copy of the report to Boyd's office, laid it on his desk. His eyes flicked down to it, then back to hers. "The cop—Barkley—he's still in surgery. The woman's out of danger."

"Good. How's the kid?"

"She has an aunt in Colorado Springs. Social Services contacted her. The creep was her father. History of battering and drugs. His wife took the kid about a year ago and went to a women's shelter. Filed for divorce. She moved here about three months ago, got herself a job, started a life."

"And he found her."

"And he found her."

"Well, he won't find her again." She turned toward the door, but Boyd was up and walking around the desk. "Thea." He shut the door, cutting off most of the din from the bull pen. "Are you okay?"

"Sure. I don't see IAD hassling me on this one."

"I'm not talking about Internal Affairs." He tilted his head. "A day or two off wouldn't hurt."

"It wouldn't help, either." She lifted her shoulders, let them fall. To Boyd she could say things she could never say to anyone else. "I didn't think I'd get to her in time. I didn't get to her," she added. "Colt did. And he shouldn't have been there."

"He was there." Gently Boyd laid his hands on her shoulders. "Oh-oh, it's the supercop complex. I can see it coming. Dodging bullets, filing reports, screaming down dark alleys, selling tickets to the Policemen's Ball, ridding the world of bad guys and saving cats from the tops of trees. She can do it all."

"Shut up, Fletcher." But she smiled. "I draw the line at saving cats."

"Want to come to dinner tonight?"

She rested a hand on the knob. "What's to eat?"

He shrugged, grinned. "Can't say. It's Maria's night off."

"Cilla's cooking?" She gave him a pained, sorrowful look. "I thought we were friends."

"We'll send out for tacos."

"Deal."

When she walked back into the bull pen, she spotted Colt. He had his boots up on a desk and a phone at his ear. She strolled over, sat on the corner and waited for him to finish the call.

"Paperwork done?" he asked her.

"Nightshade, I don't suppose I have to point out that this desk, this phone, this chair, are department property, and off-limits to civilians."

He grinned at her. "Nope. But go right ahead, if you want to. You look good enough to eat when you're spouting proper procedure."

"Why, your compliments just take my breath away." She knocked his feet off the desk. "The stolen car's been impounded. The lab boys are going over it, so I don't see the point in rushing to take a look."

"Got a different plan?"

"Starting with the Tick Tock, I'm going to hit a few of Wild Bill's hangouts, talk to some people."

"I'm with you."

"Don't rub it in."

When she started toward the garage, he took her arm. "My car this time, remember?"

With a shrug, she went with him out to the street. His rugged black four-wheeler had a parking ticket on the windshield. Colt stuffed it in his pocket. "I don't suppose I can ask you to fix this."

"No." Althea climbed in.

"That's okay. Fletch'll do it."

She slanted him a look, and what might have been a smile, before turning to stare out of the windshield again. "You did good with that kid today." It galled her a bit to admit it, but it had to be done. "I don't think she'd have made it without you."

"Us," he said. "Some people might have called it teamwork."

She fastened her belt with a jerk of her wrist. "Some people."

"Don't take it so hard, Thea." Whistling through

his teeth, he shoved the gearshift into First and cruised into traffic. "Now, where were we before we were interrupted? Oh, yeah, you were telling me about yourself."

"I don't think so."

"Okay, I'll tell me about you. You're a woman who likes structure, depends on it. No, no, it's more that you insist on it," he said. "That's why you're so good at your job, all that law and order."

She snorted. "You should be a psychiatrist, Nightshade. Who could have guessed a cop would prefer law and order?"

"Don't interrupt, I'm on a roll. You're what— twenty-seven, twenty-eight?"

"Thirty-two. You lost your roll."

"I'll pick it up again." He glanced down at her naked ring finger. "You're not married."

"Another brilliant deduction."

"You have a tendency toward sarcasm, and an affection for wearing silk and expensive perfume. Real nice perfume, Thea, the kind that seduces a man's mind before his body gets involved."

"Maybe you should be writing ad copy."

"There's nothing subtle about your sexuality. It's just there, in big capital letters. Now, some women would exploit it, some would disguise it.

You don't do either, so I figure you've decided somewhere along the line that it's up to a man to deal with it. And that's not only smart, it's wise."

She didn't have an answer to that, he thought. Or didn't choose to give him one.

"You don't waste time, you don't waste energy. That way, when you need either one, you've got them. There's a cop's brain inside there, so you can size up a situation fast and act on it. And I figure you can handle a man every bit as coolly as you do your gun."

"An interesting analysis, Nightshade."

"You didn't flinch when you took that guy out today. It bothered you, but you didn't flinch." He pulled up in front of the Tick Tock and turned off the ignition. "If I've got to work with somebody, with the possibility of heading into a nasty situation, I like knowing she doesn't flinch."

"Well, gee, thanks. Now I can stop worrying that you don't approve of me." Her temper on the boil, she slammed out of the car.

"Finally…" Colt reached her in a few long-legged strides and swung his arm over her shoulder. "A little heat. It's a relief to see there's some temper in there, too."

She surprised them both by ramming an elbow

into his gut. "You wouldn't be relieved if I cut it loose. Take my word for it."

They spent the next two hours going from bar to pool hall to grubby diner. It wasn't until they tried a hole-in-the-wall called Clancy's that they made some progress.

The lights were dim, a sop to the early drinkers, who liked to forget that the sun was still up. A radio behind the bar scratched out country music that told a sad tale of cheating and empty bottles. Several of those early customers were already scattered at the bar or at tables, most of them doing their drinking steadily and solo.

The liquor was watered, and the glasses were dingy, but the whiskey came cheap and the atmosphere was conducive to getting seriously drunk.

Althea walked to the end of the bar and ordered a club soda she had no intention of sampling. Colt opted for the beer on tap. She lifted a brow.

"Had a tetanus shot recently?" She took out a twenty, but kept her finger on the corner of the bill as their drinks were served. "Wild Bill used to come in here pretty regular."

The bartender glanced down at the bill, and back at Althea. Bloodshot eyes and the map of broken capillaries over his broad face attested to the fact that he swallowed as much as he served.

Althea prompted him. "Wild Bill Billings."

"So?"

"He was a friend of mine."

"Looks like you lost a friend."

"I was in here with him a couple of times." Althea drew the twenty back a fraction. "Maybe you remember."

"My memory's real selective, but it don't have no trouble making a cop."

"Good. Then you probably figured out that Bill and I had an arrangement."

"I probably figured out the arrangement got him splattered all over the sidewalk."

"You'd have figured that one wrong. He wasn't snitching for me when he got hit, and me, I'm just the sentimental type. I want who did him, and I'm willing to pay." She shoved the bill forward. "A lot more than this."

"I don't know nothing about it." But the twenty disappeared into his pocket.

"But you might know people who know people who know something." She leaned forward, a smile in her eyes. "If you put the word out, I'd appreciate it."

He shrugged, and would have moved away, but she put a hand on his arm. "I think that twenty's worth a minute or two more. Bill had a girl named Jade. She's skipped. He had a couple others, didn't he?"

"A couple. He wasn't much of a pimp."

"Got a name?"

He took out a dirty rag and began to wipe the dirty bar. "A black-haired girl named Meena. She worked out of here sometimes. Haven't seen her lately."

"If you do, you give me a call." She took out a card and dropped it onto the bar. "You know anything about movies? Private movies, with young girls?"

He looked blank and shrugged, but not before Althea saw the flash of knowledge in his eyes. "I ain't got time for movies, and that's all you get for twenty."

"Thanks." Althea strolled out. "Give him a minute," she said under her breath to Colt. Then she peered through the dirty window. "Look at that. Funny that he'd get an urge to make a call just now."

Colt watched the bartender hurry to the wall phone, drop in a quarter. "I like your style, Lieutenant."

"Let's see how much you like it after a few

hours in a cold car. We've got a stakeout tonight, Nightshade."

"I'm looking forward to it."

Chapter 3

She was right about the cold. He didn't mind it so much, not with long johns and a sheepskin jacket to ward it off. But he did mind the dragging inactivity. He'd have sworn that Althea thrived on it.

She was settled comfortably in the passenger seat, working a crossword puzzle by the dim glow of the glove-compartment light. She worked methodically, patiently, endlessly, he thought, while he tried to stave off boredom with the B. B. King retrospective on the radio.

He thought of the evening they'd both missed at the Fletchers'. Hot food, blazing fire, warm brandy. It had even occurred to him that Althea might have defrosted a bit in unofficial surroundings. It might not have helped matters to think of her that way—the ice goddess melting—but it did something for his more casual fantasies.

In his current reality, she was all cop, and emotionally as distant from him as the moon. But in the daydream, assisted by the slow blues on the radio, she was all woman—seductive as the black silk he imagined her wearing, enticing as the crackling fire he pictured burning low in a stone hearth, soft as the white fur rug they lowered themselves to.

And her taste, once his mouth sampled hers, was honeyed whiskey. Drugging, sweet, potent. Her scent tangled up with her flavor in his senses until they were one and the same. An opiate a man could drown in.

The silk slipped away, inch by seductive inch, revealing the alabaster flesh beneath. Rose-petal smooth, flawless as glass, firm and soft as water. And when she reached for him, drew him in, her lips moved against his ear in whispered invitation.

"Want more coffee?"

"Huh?" He snapped back, swiveling his head around to stare at her in the shadowed car. She held a thermos out to him. "What?"

"Coffee?" Intrigued by the look on his face, she picked up his cup herself and filled it halfway. At first glance, she would have said there was temper in his eyes, ripe and ready to rip. But she knew that look, and knew it well. This was desire, equally ripe, equally ready. "Taking a side trip, Nightshade?"

"Yeah." He accepted the cup and drank deep, wishing it was whiskey. But his lips curved, his amusement with himself and the ridiculous situation easing the discomfort in his gut. "One hell of a trip."

"Well, try to keep up with our tour, will you?" She sipped from her own cup and offered him a share of her bag of candy. "There goes another one." Efficient, she set aside her cup and picked up her camera. She took two quick shots of the man entering the bar. He was only the second who had gone in during the past hour.

"They don't exactly do a thriving business down here, do they?"

"Most people like a little ambience with their liquor."

"Ferns and canned music?"

She set the camera aside again. "Clean glasses, for a start. I doubt we're going to see one of our moviemakers down here."

"Then why are we sitting in a cold car looking at a dive at eleven o'clock at night?"

"Because it's my job." She chose a single piece of candy, popped it into her mouth. "And because I'm waiting for something else."

It was the first he'd heard of it. "Want to clue me in?"

"No." She chose another piece and went back to her crossword puzzle.

"Okay, that tears it." He ripped the paper out of her hands. "You want to play games, Grayson? Let me tell you how I play. I get peeved when people hold out on me. I get especially peeved when I'm bored senseless while they're doing it. Then I get mean."

"Excuse me," she said, in a mild tone that was in direct contrast to the fire in her eyes. "I can hardly speak for the ball of terror in my throat."

"You want to be scared?" He moved fast, eerily so. She wouldn't have been able to evade him if she'd tried. So she submitted without any show of resistance when he grabbed her by the shoulders. "I figure I ought to be able to put the fear of God into you, Thea, and liven things up a bit for both of us."

"Back off. If you've finished your imitation of

machismo, what I've been waiting for is about to walk into the bar."

"What?"

He turned his head, which presented Althea with the perfect opportunity to grab his thumb and twist it viciously. When he swore, she released him. "Meena. Wild Bill's other girl." Althea lifted her camera and took another shot. "I got her picture out of the files this afternoon. She's done time. Solicitation, running a confidence game, possession with intent to sell, disorderly behavior."

"A sweet girl, our Meena."

"*Your* Meena," Althea told him. "Since you play the big, bad type so well, you can go on in and charm Meena, get her out here so we can talk." Opening her purse, Althea took out an envelope with five crisp ten-dollar bills. "And if your charm fails, offer her fifty."

"You want me to go in and convince her I'm looking to party?"

"That's the ticket."

"Fine." He'd certainly done worse in his career than play the eager john in a seedy bar. But he shoved the envelope back into her lap. "I've got my own money."

Althea watched him cross the street, waiting

until he'd disappeared inside. Then she leaned back and indulged herself for one moment by closing her eyes and letting out a long, long breath.

A dangerous man, Colt Nightshade, she thought. A deadly man. She hadn't felt simple anger when he lunged toward her and grabbed. She hadn't felt simple anything. What she'd experienced was complex, convoluted and confusing.

What she'd felt was arousal, gut-deep, red-hot, soul-searing arousal, mixed with a healthy dose of primal fear and teeth-baring fury.

It wasn't like her, she told herself as she took the time alone to gather her wits. Coming that close to losing control because a man pushed the wrong buttons—or the right ones—was uncharacteristic of her.

She pushed the buttons. That was Althea Grayson's number one hard-and-fast rule. And if Colt thought he could break that one, he was in for a big disappointment.

She'd worked too hard forming herself into what she was, laying out the stages of her life and following them. She'd come from chaos, and she'd beaten it back. Certainly it was necessary from time to time to change the pattern. She wasn't rigid. But nothing, absolutely nothing, jarred that pattern.

It was the case itself, she supposed. The child being held by strangers, almost certainly being abused.

Another pattern, she thought bitterly. All too familiar to her.

And the child that morning, she remembered. Helplessly trapped by the adults around her.

She shook that off, picked up the crumpled newspaper to fold it neatly and set it aside.

She was just tired, she told herself. The drug bust the week before had been vicious. And to tumble from that into this would have shaken anyone. What she needed was a vacation. She smiled to herself, imagining a warm white-sand beach, blue water, a tall spear of glistening hotel behind her. A big bed, room service, mud packs, and a private whirlpool.

And that was just what she was going to have when she capped this case and sent Colt Nightshade back to his cattle or his law practice or whatever the hell he called his profession.

Glancing toward the bar again, she was forced to nod in approval. Less than ten minutes had passed, and he was coming out, Meena in tow.

"Oh, a group thing?" Meena studied Althea through heavily kohled eyes. She pushed back her stiff black curls and smirked. "Well, now, honey, that's going to cost you extra."

"No problem." Gallantly Colt helped her into the back seat.

"I guess a guy like you can handle the two of us." She settled back, reeking of floral cologne.

"I don't think that'll be necessary." Althea took out her badge, flashed it.

Meena swore, shot Colt a look of intense dislike, then folded her arms. "Haven't you cops got anything better to do than roust us working girls?"

"We won't have to take you in, Meena, if you answer a few questions. Drive around a little, will you, Colt?" As he obliged, Althea turned in her seat. "Wild Bill was a friend of mine."

"Yeah, right."

"He did some favors for me. I did some for him."

"Yeah, I bet—" Meena broke off, narrowed her eyes. "You the cop he snitched for? The one he called classy?" Meena relaxed a little. There was a pretty good chance she wouldn't be spending the night in lockup after all. "He said you were okay. Said you always slipped him a few without whining about it."

Althea noted Meena's greedy little smile and

lifted a brow. "I'm touched. Maybe he should've said I paid when he had something worth buying. Do you know Jade?"

"Sure. She hasn't been around for a few weeks. Bill said she skipped town." Meena dug in her red vinyl purse and pulled out a cigarette. When Colt clicked on his lighter and offered the flame, she cupped her hand over his and slanted him a warm look under thickly blackened lashes. "Thanks, honey."

"How about this girl?" Colt took the snapshot of Elizabeth out of his pocket. After turning on the dome light, he offered it to Meena.

"No." She started to pass it back, then frowned. "I don't know. Maybe." While she considered, she blew out a stream of smoke, clouding the car. "Not on the stroll. Seems like maybe I saw her somewhere."

"With Bill?" Althea asked.

"Hell, no. Bill didn't deal in jailbait."

"Who does?"

Meena shifted her eyes to Colt. "Georgie Cool's got a few young ones in his stable. Nobody as fresh as this, though."

"Did Bill get you a gig, Meena? A movie gig?" Althea asked.

"Maybe he did."

"The answer's yes, or the answer's no." Althea took back the photo of Liz. "You waste my time, I don't waste my money."

"Well, hell, it don't bother me if some guy wants to take videos while I work. They paid extra for it."

"Have you got a name?"

Meena snorted in Althea's direction. "We didn't exchange business cards, sweetie."

"But you can give me a description. How many were involved. Where it went down."

"Probably." The sly look was back as Meena blew out smoke. "If I had some incentive."

"Your incentive's not to spend time in a cell with a two-hundred-pound Swede named Big Jane," Althea said mildly.

"You can't send me up. I'll scream entrapment."

"Scream all you want. With your record, the judge will just chuckle."

"Come on, Thea." Colt's drawl seemed to have thickened. "Give the lady a break. She's trying to cooperate. Aren't you, Meena?"

"Sure." Meena butted out her cigarette, licked her lips. "Sure I am."

"What she's trying to do is hose me." Althea realized she and Colt had picked up the good cop—

bad cop routine without missing a beat. "And I want answers."

"She's giving them to us." He smiled at Meena in the rearview mirror. "Just take your time."

"There were three of them," Meena said, and set her cherry-red lips in a pout. "The guy running the camera, another guy sitting back in a corner. I couldn't see him. And the guy who was, like, performing with me, you know? The guy with the camera was bald. A black guy, really big—like a wrestler or something. I was there about an hour, and he never opened his mouth once."

Althea flipped open her notebook. "Did they call each other by name?"

"No." Meena thought it through, shook her head. "No. That's funny, isn't it? They didn't talk to each other at all, as I remember. The one I was working with was a little guy—except for certain vital parts." She chuckled and reached for another cigarette. "Now, *he* did some talking. Trash talk, get it? Like for the camera. Some guys like that. He was, I don't know…in his forties, maybe, skinny, had his hair pulled back in a ponytail that hit his shoulder blades. He wore this Lone Ranger mask."

"I'm going to want you to work with a police artist," Althea told her.

"No way. No more cops."

"We don't have to do it at the station." Althea played her trump card. "If you give us a good enough description, one that helps us nail these film buffs, there's an extra hundred for you."

"Okay." Meena brightened. "Okay."

Althea tapped her pencil against her pad. "Where did you shoot?"

"Shoot? Oh, you mean the movie? Over on Second. Real nice place. It had one of them whirlpool tubs in the bathroom, and mirrors for walls." Meena leaned forward to brush her fingertips over Colt's shoulder. "It was…stimulating."

"The address?" Althea said.

"I don't know. One of those big condo buildings on Second. Top floor, too. Like the penthouse."

"I bet you'd recognize the building if we drove by it, wouldn't you, Meena?" Colt's tone was all friendly encouragement, as was the smile he shot her over his shoulder.

"Yeah, sure I would."

And she did. Minutes later she was pointing out the window. "That place, there. See the one up top, with the big windows and the balcony thing? It was in there. Real class joint. White carpet. This really sexy bedroom, with red curtains and a big round bed. There was gold faucets in the bathroom, shaped like swans. Jeez. I woulda loved to go back."

"You only went once?" Colt asked her.

"Yeah. They told Billy I wasn't the right type." With a sound of disgust, she reached for yet another cigarette. "Get this. I was too old. I just had my twenty-second birthday, and those creeps tell Billy I'm too old. It really ticked me— Oh, yeah…" Suddenly inspired, she rapped Colt on the shoulder. "The kid. The one in the picture? That's where I saw her. I was leaving, but I went back 'cause I left my smokes. She was sitting in the kitchen. I didn't recognize her in the picture right off, 'cause she was all made-up when I saw her."

"Did she say anything to you?" Colt asked, struggling to keep his voice quiet and even. "Do anything?"

"No, just sat there. She looked stoned to me."

Because she sensed he needed something, Althea slid her hand across the seat and covered Colt's. His was rigid. She was surprised, but didn't protest, when he turned his hand over and gripped hers, palm to palm.

"I'm going to want to talk to you again." With

her free hand, Althea reached into her purse for enough money to ensure Meena's continued cooperation. "I need a number where I can reach you."

"No sweat." Meena rattled it off while she counted her money. "I guess Billy had it right. You're square. Hey, maybe you could drop me at the Tick Tock. I think I'll go in and drink one for Wild Bill."

"We can't do anything without a warrant." Althea was repeating the statement for the third time as they stepped out of the elevator on the top floor of the building Meena had pointed out.

"You don't need a warrant to knock on a door."

"Right." With a sigh, Althea slipped a hand inside her jacket in an automatic check of her weapon. "And they're going to invite us in for coffee. If you give me a couple of hours—"

When he whirled, her jaw dropped. After the cool, matter-of-fact manner in which he'd handled everything up to this point, the raw fury on his face was staggering. "Get this, Lieutenant—I'm not waiting another two *minutes* to see if Liz is in there. And if she is, if anybody is, I'm not going to need a damn warrant."

"Look, Colt, I understand—"

"You don't understand diddley."

She opened her mouth, then shut it again, shocked that she'd been about to shout that she did understand. Oh, yes, she understood very, very well. "We'll knock," she said tightly, and strode to the door of the penthouse and did so.

"Maybe they're hard of hearing." Colt used his fist to hammer. When the summons went unanswered, he moved so fast Althea didn't have time to swear. He'd already kicked the door in.

"Good, real good, Nightshade. Subtle as a brick."

"Guess I slipped." He pulled his gun out of his boot. "And look at this, the door's open."

"Don't—" But he was already inside. Cursing Boyd and all his boyhood friends, Althea drew her weapon and went in the door behind him, instinctively covering his back. She didn't need the light Colt turned on to see that the room was empty. It had a deserted feel. There was nothing left but the carpet, and the drapes at the windows.

"Split," Colt muttered to himself as he moved quickly from room to room. "The bastards split."

Satisfied she wouldn't need it, Althea replaced her gun. "I guess we know who our friendly bartender called this afternoon. We'll see what we

can get from the rental contract, the neighbors…"
Yet she thought if their quarry had been this slick
so far, what they got would be close to useless.

She stepped into the bathroom. It was as Meena
had described, the big black whirlpool tub, the
swan-shaped faucets—brass, not gold—the all-
around mirrors. "You've just jeopardized the integ-
rity of a possible crime scene, Nightshade. I hope
you're satisfied."

"She could have been here," he said from behind her.

She looked over, saw their reflections trapped in
the mirrored tiles. It was the expression on his face,
one she hadn't expected to see there, that softened
her. "We're going to find her, Colt," she said quietly. "We're going to see that she gets back home."

"Sure." He wanted to break something, anything. It took every ounce of his will not to smash
his fist through the mirrors. "Every day they've got
her is a day she's going to have to live with, forever." Bending, he slipped his gun back in his boot.
"God, Thea, she's just a child."

"Children are tougher than most people think.
They close things off when they have to. And it's
going to be easier because she has family who
loves her."

"Easier than what?"

Than having no one but yourself, she thought. "Just easier." She couldn't help it. She reached out, laid a hand on his cheek. "Don't let it eat at you, Colt. You'll mess up if you do."

"Yeah." He drew it back, that dangerous emotion that led to dangerous mistakes. But when she started to drop her hand and move past him, Colt snagged her wrist. "You know something?" Maybe it was only because he needed contact, but he tugged her an inch closer. "For a minute there, you were almost human."

"Really?" Their bodies were almost brushing. A bad move, she thought. But it would be cowardly to pull back. "What am I usually?"

"Perfect." He lifted his free hand—because he'd wanted to almost from the first moment he'd seen her—and tangled his fingers in her hair. "It's scary," he said. "It's the whole package—that face, the hair, the body, the mind. A man doesn't know whether to bay at the moon or whimper at your feet."

She had to tilt her head back to keep her eyes level with his. If her heart was beating a bit faster, she could ignore it. It had happened before. If she felt the little pull of curiosity, even of lust, it wasn't the first time, and it could be controlled. But what was difficult, very difficult, to channel, was the unexpected clouding of her senses. That would have to be fought.

"You don't strike me as the type to do either," she said, and smiled, a cool, tight-lipped smirk that had most men backing off babbling.

Colt wasn't most men.

"I never have been. Why don't we try something else?" He said it slowly, then moved like lightning to close his mouth over hers.

If she had protested, if she had struggled—if there had been even a token pulling back—he would have released her and counted his losses. Maybe.

But she didn't. That surprised them both.

She could have, should have. She would think later. She could have stopped him cold with any number of defensive or offensive moves. She would think later. But there was such raw heat in his lips, such steely strength in his arms, such whirling pleasure in her own body.

Oh, yes, she would think later. Much later.

It was exactly as he'd imagined it. And he'd imagined it a lot. That tart, flamboyant flavor she carried on her lips was the twin of the one he'd sampled in his mind. It was as addicting as any opiate. When she opened for him, he dived deeper and took more.

She was as small, as slim, as supple, as any man could wish. And as strong. Her arms were locked hard around him, and her fingers were clutching at his hair. The low, deep sound of approval that vibrated in her throat had his blood racing like a fast-moving river.

Murmuring her name, he spun her around, ramming her against the mirrors, covering her body with his. His hands ran over her in a greedy sprint to take and touch and possess. Then his fingers were jerking at the buttons on her blouse in a desperate need to push aside the first barrier.

He wanted her now. No, no, he needed her now, he realized. The way a man needed sleep after a vicious day of hard labor, the way he needed to eat after a long, long fast.

He tore his mouth from hers to press it against her throat, reveling in the sumptuous taste of flesh.

Half-delirious, she arched back, moaning at the thrill of his hungry mouth on her heated skin. Without the wall for support, she knew, she would already have sunk to the floor. And it was there, just there, that he would take her, that they would take each other. On the cool, hard tile, with dozens of mirrors tossing back reflections of their desperate bodies.

Here and now.

And like a thief sneaking into a darkened house, an image of Meena, and what had gone on in that apartment, crept into her mind.

What was she doing? Good Lord, what was she *doing?* she raged at herself as she levered herself away.

She was a cop, and she had been about to indulge in some wild bout of mindless sex in the middle of a crime scene.

"Stop!" Her voice was harsh with arousal and self-disgust. "I mean it, Colt. Stop. Now."

"What?" Like a diver surfacing from fathoms-deep, he shook his head, nearly swayed. Good Lord, his knees were weak. To compensate, he braced a hand on the wall as he stared down at her. He'd loosened her hair, and it spilled rich and red over her shoulders. Her eyes were more gold than brown now, huge, and seductively misted. Her mouth was full, reddened by the pressure and demand of his, and her skin was flushed a pale, lovely rose.

"You're beautiful. Impossibly beautiful." Gently he skimmed a finger down her throat. "Like some exotic flower behind glass. A man just has to break that glass and take it."

"No." She grabbed his hand to keep from losing her mind again. "This is insane, completely insane."

"Yeah." He couldn't have agreed more. "And it felt great."

"This is an investigation, Nightshade. And we're standing in what is very possibly the scene of a major crime."

He smiled and lifted her hand to nip at her fingers. Just because this was a dead end for their investigation didn't mean all activity had to come to a halt. "So, let's go someplace else."

"We are going someplace else." She shoved him away, and quickly, competently redid her blouse. "Separately." She wasn't steady, she realized. Damn him, damn her, she wasn't steady.

He felt that the safest place for his hands at the moment, was his pockets so he shoved them in. She was right, one hundred percent right, and that was the worst of it.

"You want to pretend this didn't happen?"

"I don't pretend anything." Settling on dignity, she pushed her tumbled hair back, smoothed down her rumpled jacket. "It happened, now it's done."

"Not by a long shot, Lieutenant. We're both grown-ups, and though I can only speak for myself, that kind of connection just doesn't happen every day."

"You're right." She inclined her head. "You can only speak for yourself." She made it back to the living room before he grabbed her arm and spun her around to face him.

"You want me to press the point now?" His voice was quiet, deadly quiet. "Or do you want to be straight with me?"

"All right, fine." She could be honest, because lies wouldn't work. "If I were interested in a quick, hot affair, I'd certainly give you a call. As it happens, I have other priorities at the moment."

"You've got a list, right?"

She had to take a moment to get her temper back under wraps. "Do you think that insults me?" she asked sweetly. "I happen to prefer organizing my life."

"Compartmentalizing."

She arched a brow. "Whatever. For better or worse, we have a professional relationship. I want that girl found, Colt, every bit as much as you do. I want her back with her family, eating hamburgers and worrying over her latest math test. And I want to bring down the bastards who have her. More than you could possibly understand."

"Then why don't you help me understand?"

"I'm a cop," she told him. "That's enough."

"No, it's not." There had been passion in her face, the same kind of passion he'd felt when he had her in his arms. Fierce and ragged and at the edge of control. "Not for you, or for me, either."

He let out a deep breath and rubbed the base of his neck, where most of his tension had lodged. They were both tired, he realized, tired and strung out. It wasn't the time and it wasn't the place to delve into personal reasons. He'd need to find some objectivity if he wanted to figure out Althea Grayson.

"Look, I'd apologize for back there if I was out of line. But we both know I wasn't. I'm here to get Liz back, and nothing's going to stop me. And after a taste of you, Thea, I'm going to be just as determined to have more."

"I'm not the soup du jour, Nightshade," she said wearily. "You'll only get what I give."

His grin flashed, quick and easy. "That's just the way I want it. Come on, I'll drive you home."

Saying nothing, Althea stared after him. She had the uncomfortable feeling that they hadn't resolved matters precisely as she'd wanted.

Chapter 4

Armed with a second cup of coffee, Colt stood at the edge of a whirlwind. It was obvious to him that getting three kids out of the house and onto a school bus was an event of major proportions. He could only wonder how a trio of adults could handle the orchestration on a daily basis and remain sane.

"I don't like this cereal," Bryant complained. He lifted a spoonful and, scowling, let the soggy mess plop back into his bowl. "It tastes like wet trees."

"You picked it out, because it had a whistle inside," Cilla reminded him as she slapped peanut-butter-and-jelly sandwiches together. "You eat it."

"Put a banana on it," Boyd suggested while he struggled to bundle Allison's pale, flyaway hair into something that might have passed for a braid.

"Ouch! Daddy, you're pulling!"

"Sorry. What's the capital of Nebraska?"

"Lincoln," his daughter said with a sigh. "I hate geography tests." While she pouted over it, she practiced her pliés for ballet class. "How come I have to know the stupid states and their stupid capitals, anyway?"

"Because knowledge is sacred." With his tongue caught in his teeth, Boyd fought to band the wispy braid. "And once you learn something, you never really forget it."

"Well, I can't remember the capital of Virginia."

"It's, ah…" As the sacred knowledge escaped him, Boyd swore under his breath. What the hell did he care? He lived in Colorado. One of the major problems with having kids, as he saw it, was that the parents were forced to go back to school. "It'll come to you."

"Mom, Bry's feeding Bongo his cereal." Allison sent her brother a smug, smarmy smile of the kind that only a sister can achieve.

Cilla turned in time to see her son thrusting his

spoon toward their dog's eager mouth. "Bryant Fletcher, you're going to be wearing that cereal in a minute."

"But look, Mom, even Bongo won't eat it. It's crap."

"Don't say 'crap,'" Cilla told him wearily. But she noted that the big, scruffy dog, who regularly drank out of toilet bowls, had turned up his nose after one sample of soggy Rocket Crunchies. "Eat the banana, and get your coat."

"Mom!" Keenan, the youngest, scrambled into the room. He was shoeless and sockless, and was holding one grubby high-top sneaker in his hand. "I can't find my other shoe. It's not anywhere. Somebody musta stole it."

"Call a cop," Cilla muttered as she dumped the last peanut-butter-and-jelly sandwich into a lunch box.

"I'll find it, *señora*." Maria wiped her hands on her apron.

"Bless you."

"Bad guys took it, Maria," Keenan told her, his voice low and serious. "They came in the middle of the night and swiped it. Daddy'll go out and lock them up."

"Of course he will." Equally sober, Maria took

his hand to lead him toward the stairs. "Now we go look for clues, *sí?*"

"Umbrellas." Cilla turned from the counter, running a hand through her short crop of brown hair. "It's raining. Do we have umbrellas?"

"We used to have umbrellas." His hairstyling duties completed, Boyd poured himself another cup of coffee. "Somebody stole them. Probably the same gang who stole Keenan's shoe and Bryant's spelling homework. I've already put a task force on it."

"Big help you are." Cilla went to the kitchen doorway. "Maria! Umbrellas!" She turned back, tripping over the dog, swore, then grabbed three lunch boxes. "Coats," she ordered. "You've got five minutes to make the bus."

There was a mad scramble, impeded by Bongo, who decided this was the perfect time to jump on everyone in sight.

"He hates goodbyes," Boyd told Colt as he deftly collared the mutt.

"The shoe was in the closet," Maria announced as she hustled Keenan into the kitchen.

"The thieves must have hidden it there. It's too diabolical." She offered him his lunch box. "Kiss."

Keenan grinned and planted a loud smack on her lips. "I get to be the milk monitor all week."

"It's a tough job, but I know you're up to it. Bry, the banana peel goes in the trash." As she handed him his lunch box, she hooked an arm around his throat, making him giggle as she kissed him good-bye. "Allison, the capital of Virginia's Richmond. I think."

"Okay."

After everyone exchanged kisses—including, Colt noted with some amusement, Bongo—Cilla held up one hand.

"Anyone leaving his or her umbrella at school will be immediately executed. Scram."

They all bolted. The door slammed. Cilla closed her eyes. "Ah, another quiet morning at the Fletchers'. Colt what can I offer you? Bacon, eggs? Whiskey?"

"I'll take the first two. Reserve the last." Grinning, he took the chair Bryant had vacated. "You put on this show every day?"

"With matinees on Saturdays." She ruffled her hair again, checked the clock on the stove. "I'd like to hang around with you guys, but I've got to get ready for work. I've got a meeting in an hour. If you find yourself at loose ends, Colt, stop by the radio station. I'll show you around."

"I might just do that."

"Maria, do you need me to pick up anything?"

"No, *señora*." She already had the bacon sizzling. *"Gracias."*

"I should be home by six." Cilla paused by the table to run a hand over her husband's shoulder. "I hear there's a big poker game here tonight."

"That's the rumor." Boyd tugged his wife down to him, and Colt saw their lips curve before they met. "You taste pretty good, O'Roarke."

"Strawberry jelly. Catch you later, Slick." She gave him one last, lingering kiss before she left him.

Colt listened to her race up the stairs. "You hit the bull's-eye, didn't you, Fletch?"

"Hmm?"

"Terrific wife, great kids. And the first time out."

"Looks that way. I guess I knew Cilla was it for me almost from the first." Remembering made him smile. "Took a little while to convince her she couldn't live without me, though."

It was tough not to envy that particular smile, Colt mused. "You and Althea, you were partners when you met Cilla, right?"

"Yeah. All three of us were working nights in those days. Thea was the first woman I'd ever partnered with. Turned out to be the best cop I'd ever partnered with, as well."

"I have to ask—you don't have to answer, but I have to ask." And how best to pose the question? Colt wondered as he picked up a fork and tapped it on the edge of the table. "You and Thea…before Cilla, there was nothing…personal?"

"There's plenty personal when you're partners, working together, sometimes around the clock." He picked up his coffee, his smile easy. "But there was nothing romantic, if that's what you're dancing around."

"It's none of my business." Colt shrugged, annoyed by just how much Boyd's answer relieved him. "I was curious."

"Curious why I didn't try to move in on a woman with her looks? Her brains? Her—what's the best word for it?" Amused by Colt's obvious discomfort, he chuckled as Maria silently served their breakfast. "Thanks, Maria. We'll call it style, for lack of something better. It's simple, Colt. I'm not going to say I didn't think about it. Could be Thea gave it a couple moments of her time, too. But we clicked as partners, we clicked as friends, and it just didn't take us down any of those other alleys." He scooped up some eggs, arched a brow. "You thinking about it?"

Colt moved his shoulders again, toyed with his

bacon. "I can't say we've clicked as partners—or as friends, for that matter. But I figure we've already turned down one of those other alleys."

Boyd didn't pretend to be surprised. Anyone who said oil and water didn't mix just hadn't stirred them up enough. "There are some women who get under your skin, some that get into your head. And some who do both."

"Yeah. So what's the story on her?"

"She's a good cop, a person you can trust. Like anybody else, she's got some baggage, but she carries it well. If you want to know personal stuff, you'll have to ask her." He lifted his cup. "And she'd get the same answer from me about you."

"Has she asked?"

"Nope." Boyd sipped to hide his grin. "Now, why don't you tell me your progress in finding Liz?"

"We got a tip on the place on Second Avenue, but they'd already split." It still frustrated him. The whole bloody business frustrated him. "Figured I'd talk to the apartment manager, the neighbors. There's a witness who might be able to ID one or more of our movie moguls."

"That's a good start. Anything I can do to help?"

"I'll let you know. They've already had her a

couple of weeks, Fletch. I'm going to get her back." He lifted his gaze, and the quiet rage in it left no room for doubt. "What worries me is what shape she'll be in when I do."

"Take it one step at a time."

"That sounds like the lieutenant." Colt preferred to take leaps, rather than steps. "I can't hook up with her until later this afternoon. She's in court or something."

"In court?" Boyd frowned, then nodded. "Right. The Marsten trial. Armed robbery, assault. She made a good collar on that one. Do you want me to send a uniform with you to Second Avenue?"

"No. I'd just as soon handle it myself."

It was good to be back on his own, Colt decided. Working alone meant you didn't have to worry about stepping on your partner's toes or debating strategy. And as far as Althea was concerned, it meant he didn't have to work overtime trying to keep himself from thinking of her as a woman.

First he rousted the apartment manager, Nieman, a short, balding man who obviously thought his position required him to wear a three-piece suit, a brutally knotted tie, and an ocean of pine-scented after-shave.

"I've already given my statement to the other officer," he informed Colt through the two-inch crack provided by the security chain on his door.

"Now you'll have to give it to me." Colt saw no need to disabuse Nieman of the notion that he was with the police. "Do you want me to shout my questions from out in the hall, Mr. Nieman?"

"No." Nieman shot the chain back, clearly annoyed. "Haven't I already had enough trouble? I was hardly out of my bed this morning before you people were banging on my door. Now the phone has been ringing off the hook with tenants calling, demanding to know what the police are doing sealing off the penthouse. The resulting publicity will take weeks for me to defuse."

"You got a real tough job, Mr. Nieman." Colt scanned the apartment as he entered. It wasn't as plush or as large as the empty penthouse, but it would do in a pinch. Nieman had furnished it in fussy French rococo. Colt knew his mother would have adored it.

"You can't imagine it." Resigned, Nieman gestured toward an ornately carved chair. "Tenants are such children, really. They need someone to guide them, someone to slap their hands when they break the rules. I've been a resident apartment manager for ten years, three in this building, and the stories I could tell…"

Because Colt was afraid he would do just that, he cut Nieman off. "Why don't you tell me about the penthouse tenants?"

"There's very little I can tell." Nieman plucked at the knees of his slacks before sitting. He crossed his legs at the ankles and revealed patterned argyle socks. "As I explained to the other detective, I never actually met them. They were only here four months."

"Don't you show the apartment to tenants, Mr. Nieman? Take their applications?"

"As a rule, certainly. In this particular case, the tenant sent references and a certified check for first and last month's rent via the mail."

"Is it usual for you to rent an apartment that way?"

"Not usual, no…" After clearing his throat, Nieman fiddled with the knot of his tie. "The letter was followed up with a phone call. Mr. Davis—the tenant—explained that he was a friend of Mr. and Mrs. Ellison. They had the penthouse before, for three years. Lovely couple, elegant taste. They moved to Boston. As he'd been acquainted with them, he had no need to view the apartment. He claimed to have attended several dinner parties and other affairs in the penthouse. He was quite anxious to have it, you see, and as his references were impeccable…"

"You checked them out?"

"Of course." Lips pursed, Nieman drew himself up. "I take my responsibilities seriously."

"What did this Davis do for a living?"

"He's an engineer with a local firm. When I contacted the firm, they had nothing but the highest regard for him."

"What firm?"

"I still have the file out." Nieman reached to the coffee table for a slim folder. "Foxx Engineering," he began, then recited the address and phone number. "Naturally, I contacted his landlord, as well. We apartment managers have a code of ethics. I was assured that Mr. Davis was an ideal tenant, quiet, responsible, tidy, and that his rent was always timely. This proved to be the case."

"But you never actually saw Mr. Davis?"

"This is a large building. There are several tenants I don't see. It's the troublemakers you meet regularly, and Mr. Davis was never any trouble."

Never any trouble, Colt thought grimly as he completed the slow process of door-to-door. He carried with him copies of the lease, the references, and Davis's letter. It was past noon, and he'd already interviewed most of the tenants who'd answered his knock. Only three of them claimed to have seen the mysterious Mr. Davis. Colt now had three markedly different descriptions to add to his file.

The police seal on the penthouse door had barred his entrance. He could have picked the lock and cut the tape, but he'd doubted he'd find anything worthwhile.

So he'd started at the top and was working his way down. He was currently canvassing the third floor, with a vicious case of frustration and the beginnings of a headache.

He knocked at 302 and felt himself being sized up through the peephole. The chain rattled, the bolt turned. Now he was being sized up, face-to-face, by an old woman with a wild mop of hair dyed an improbable orange. She had bright blue eyes that sprayed into dozens of wrinkles as she squinted to peer at him. Her Denver Broncos sweatshirt was the size of a tent, covering what Colt judged to be two hundred pounds of pure bulk. She had two chins and was working on a third.

"You're too good-looking to be selling something I don't want."

"No, ma'am." If Colt had had a hat, he'd have tipped it. "I'm not selling anything at all. The police are conducting an investigation. I'd like to ask you a few questions regarding some of your neighbors in the building."

"Are you a cop? You'd have a badge if you were."

It looked as though she were a great deal sharper than Nieman. "No, ma'am, I'm not a cop. I'm working privately."

"A detective?" The blue eyes brightened like light bulbs. "Like Sam Spade? I swear, that Humphrey Bogart was the sexiest man ever born. If I'd have been Mary Astor, I wouldn't have thought twice about some dumb bird when I could have had him."

"No, ma'am." It took Colt a moment, but he finally caught on to her reference to *The Maltese Falcon*. "I kind of went for Lauren Bacall, myself. They sure did set things humming in *The Big Sleep*."

Pleased, she let out a loud, lusty laugh. "Damned if they didn't. Well, come on in. No use standing here in the doorway."

Colt entered and immediately had to start dodging furniture and cats. The apartment was packed with both. Tables, chairs, lamps, some of them superior antiques, others yard-sale rejects, were set helter-skelter throughout the wide living room. Half a dozen cats of all descriptions were curled, draped and stretched out with equal abandon.

"I collect," she told him, then plopped herself down on a Louis XV love seat. Her girth took up three-quarters of the cushions, so Colt wisely chose a ratty armchair with a faded pattern of colonial soldiers fighting redcoats. "I'm Esther Mavis."

"Colt Nightshade." Colt took it philosophically when a lean gray cat sprang into his lap and another leapt onto a wing of the chair to sniff at his hair.

"Well, just what are we investigating, Mr. Nightshade?"

"We're doing a check on the tenant who occupied the penthouse."

"The one who just moved out?" She scratched one of her chins. "Saw a bunch of burly men carrying stuff out to a van yesterday."

So had several other people, Colt thought. No

one had bothered to note whether the van had carried the name of a moving company.

"Did you notice what kind of van, Mrs. Mavis?"

"Miss," she told him. "A big one. They didn't act like any movers I ever saw."

"Oh?"

"They worked fast. Not like people who get paid by the hour. You know. Moved out some good pieces, too." Her bright eyes scanned her living room. "I like furniture. There was this Belker table I'd have liked to get my hands on. Don't know where I'd put it, but I always find room."

"Could you describe any of the movers?"

"Don't notice men unless there's something special about them." She winked slyly.

"How about Mr. Davis? Did you ever see him?"

"Can't say for sure. I don't know most of the people in the building by name. Me and my cats keep to ourselves. What did he do?"

"We're looking into it."

"Playing it close to the vest, huh? Well, Bogey would've done the same. So, he's moved out?"

"It looks that way."

"I guess I won't be able to give him his package, then."

"Package?"

"Just came yesterday. Messenger brought it, dropped it here by mistake. Davis, Mavis…" She shook her head. "People don't pay enough attention to details these days."

"I know what you mean." Colt cautiously plucked a cat from his shoulder. "What sort of a package, Miss Mavis?"

"A package package." With a few grunts and whistles, she hauled herself to her feet. "Put it back in the bedroom. Meant to take it up to him today." She moved with a kind of tanklike grace through the narrow passages between the furniture and came back with a sealed, padded bag.

"Ma'am, I'd like to take that with me. If you have a problem with that, you can call Captain Boyd Fletcher, Denver PD."

"No skin off my nose." She handed Colt the package. "Maybe when you've cracked the case, you'll come let me know what's what."

"I'll just do that." On impulse, he took out the photo of Liz. "Have you seen this girl?"

Miss Mavis looked at it, frowned over it, then shook her head. "No, not that I recollect. Is she in trouble?"

"Yes, ma'am."

"Does it have something to do with upstairs?"

"I think so."

She handed the photo back. "She's a pretty little thing. I hope you find her real soon."

"So do I."

It wasn't his usual operating procedure. Colt couldn't have said why he made the exception, why he felt he had to. Instead of opening the package and dealing with its contents immediately, he left it sealed and drove to the courthouse.

He was just in time to hear the defense's cross of Althea. She was dressed in a rust-colored suit that should have been dull. Instead, the effect was subtly powerful, with her vibrant hair twisted up off her neck and a single strand of pearls at her throat.

Colt took a seat at the back of the courtroom and watched as she competently, patiently and devastatingly ripped the defense to shreds. She never raised her voice, never stumbled over words. Anyone looking or listening, including the jury, would have judged her a cool, detached professional.

And so she was, Colt mused as he stretched out his legs and waited. Certainly no one watching her now would imagine her flaming like a rocket in a man's arms. His arms.

No one would picture this tidy, controlled woman arching and straining as a man's hands—his hands—raced over her.

But he was damned if he could forget it.

And studying her now, when she was unaware of him and completely focused on the job at hand, he began to notice other things, little things.

She was tired. He could see it in her eyes. Now and again there was the faintest whisper of impatience in her voice as she was called on to repeat herself. She shifted, crossing her legs. It was a smooth movement, economical, as always. But he sensed something else beneath it. Not nerves, he realized. Restlessness. She wanted this over with.

When the cross was complete, the judge called for a fifteen-minute recess. She winced as the gavel struck. It was just a flicker of a movement across her face, but he caught it.

Jack Holmsby caught her arm before she could move by him. "Nice job, Thea."

"Thanks. You shouldn't have any trouble nailing him."

"I'm not worried about it." He shifted, just enough to block her path. "Listen, I'm sorry things didn't work out the other night. Why don't we give it another shot? Say, dinner tomorrow night, just you and me?"

She waited a beat, not so much amazed by his gall as fatigued by it. "Jack, do the words *no way in hell* have any meaning for you?"

He only laughed and gave her arm an intimate little squeeze. For one wild moment, she considered decking him and taking the rap for assault.

"Come on, Althea. I'd like a chance to make it up to you."

"Jack, we both know you'd like a chance to make me. And it isn't going to happen. Now let go of my arm while we're both on the same side of the law."

"There's no need to be—"

"Lieutenant?" Colt drawled out the word. He let his gaze sweep over Holmsby. "Got a minute?"

"Nightshade." It annoyed the hell out of her that he'd witnessed the little tussle. "Excuse me, Jack. I've got work to do."

She strode out of the courtroom, leaving Colt to follow. "If you've got something that's worth my time, spill it," she ordered. "I'm not real pleased with lawyers at the moment."

"Darling, I don't have any briefs with me—except the ones I'm wearing."

"You're a riot, Nightshade."

"You look like a lady who could use a laugh." He took her arm, and felt his own temper peak when she stiffened. Battling it down, he steered her toward the doors. "My car's out front. Why don't we take a ride while we catch up?"

"Fine. I walked over from the precinct. You can take me back."

"Right." He found another ticket on his windshield. Not surprising, since he'd parked in a restricted zone. He pocketed it, and climbed in. "Sorry I interrupted your mating ritual."

"Kiss my butt." She snapped her seat belt into place.

"Lieutenant, I've been dreaming of doing just that." Reaching over, he popped open the glove compartment. This time she didn't stiffen at the contact, only seemed to withdraw. "Here."

"What?" She glanced down at the bottle of aspirin.

"For your headache."

"I'm fine." It wasn't exactly a lie, she thought. What she had couldn't be termed a mere headache. It was more like a freight train highballing behind her eyes.

"I hate a martyr."

"Leave me alone." She closed her eyes and effectively cut him off.

She was far from fine. She hadn't slept. Over the years, she'd become accustomed to rolling on two or three hours a night. But last night she hadn't slept at all, and she was too proud to lay the blame where it belonged. Right at Colt's door.

She'd thought of him. And she'd berated herself. She'd run over the impossible scene in the penthouse, and she'd ached. Then she'd berated herself again. She'd tried a hot bath, a boring book, yoga, warm brandy. Nothing had done the trick.

So she'd tossed and turned, and eventually she'd crawled out of bed to roam restlessly through her apartment. And she'd watched the sun come up.

Since dawn, she'd worked. It was now slightly past one, and she'd been on the job for nearly eight hours without a break. And what made it worse, what made it next to intolerable, was that she could very well be stuck with Colt for another eight.

She opened her eyes again when he stopped with a jerk of brakes. They were parked in front of a convenience store.

"I need something," he muttered, and slammed out.

Fine, terrific, she thought, and shut her eyes

again. Don't bother to ask if maybe *I* need something. Like a chain saw to slice off my head, for instance.

She heard him coming back. Odd, she mused, that she recognized the sound of his stride, the click of his boot heels, after so short a time. In defense, or simply out of obstinacy, she kept her eyes shut.

"Here." He pushed something against her hand. "Tea," he told her when she opened her eyes to stare down at the paper cup. "To wash down the aspirin." He popped the top on the bottle himself and shook out the medication. "Now take the damn pills, Althea. And eat this. You probably haven't eaten anything all day, unless it's chocolate bits or candied nuts. I've never seen a woman pick her way through a pound bag of candy the way you do."

"Sugar's loaded with energy." But she took the pills, and the tea. The package of cheese and crackers earned a frown. "Didn't they have any cupcakes?"

"You need protein."

"There's probably protein in cupcakes." The tea was too strong, and quite bitter, but it helped nonetheless. "Thanks." She sipped again, then broke down and opened the package of crackers. It was important to remember that she was responsible for her own actions, her own reactions and her own emotions. If she hadn't slept, it was her own problem. "The lab boys should have finished at the penthouse by now."

"They have. I've been there."

She muttered over a mouthful. "I'd rather you didn't go off on your own."

"I can't please everybody, so I please myself. I talked to the little weasel who manages the place. He never set eyes on the top-floor tenant."

While Althea chewed her way through the impromptu meal, he filled her in.

"I knew about Davis," she told him when he finished. "I got Nieman out of bed this morning. Already called the references. Phone disconnect on both. There is no Foxx Engineering at that address, or at any other address in Denver. Same for the apartment Davis used as a reference. Mr. and Mrs. Ellison, the former tenants, have never heard of him."

"You've been busy." Watching her, he tapped a finger on the steering wheel. "What was that you meant about not going off on your own?"

She smiled a little. The headache was backing

off. "I carry a badge," she said, deadpan. "You don't."

"Your badge didn't get you into Miss Mavis's apartment."

"Should it have?"

"I think so." Darkly pleased to be one up on her, Colt reached into the back and showed Althea the package. "Messenger delivered it to the cat lady by mistake."

"Cat lady?"

"You had to be there. Uh-uh." He snatched it out of reach as she made a move toward it. "My take, darling. I'm willing to share."

Her temper spiked, then leveled off when she noticed that the package was still intact. "It's still sealed."

"Seemed fair," he said, meeting her eyes. "I figured we should open it together."

"Looks like you figured right this time. Let's have a look."

Colt reached down and drew a knife out of his boot. As he slit open the package, Althea narrowed her eyes.

"I don't think that toy's under the legal limit, champ."

"Nope," he said easily, and slid the knife back

into his boot. Reaching into the package, he pulled out a videotape and a single sheet of paper.

Final edit. Okay for dupes? Heavy snows expected by weekend. Supplies good. Next drop send extra tapes and beer. Roads may be closed.

Althea held the sheet by a corner, then dug a plastic bag out of her purse. "We'll have it checked for prints. We could get lucky."

"It might tell us who. It won't tell us where." Colt slid the tape back into the bag. "Want to go to the movies?"

"Yeah." Althea set the bag on her lap, tapped it. "But I think this one calls for a private screening. I've got a VCR at home."

She also had a comfortable couch crowded with cushy pillows. Gleaming hardwood floors were accented by Navaho rugs. The art deco prints on the walls should have been at odds with the southwestern touches, but they weren't. Neither were the homey huddle of lush green plants on the curvy iron tea cart, the two goldfish swimming in a tube-shaped aquarium, or the footstool fashioned to resemble a squat, grinning gnome.

"Interesting place" was the best Colt could do.

"It does the job." She walked to a chrome-and-glass entertainment center, stepping out of her shoes on the way.

Colt decided that single gesture told him more about Althea Grayson than a dozen in-depth reports would have.

With her usual efficiency, she popped in the tape and flicked both the VCR and TV on.

There was no need to fast-forward past the FBI warning, because there wasn't one. After a five-second lag, the tape faded from gray.

And the show began.

Even for a man with Colt's experience, it was a surprise. He tucked his hands in his pockets and rocked back on his heels. It was foolish, he supposed, seeing as they were both adults, both professionals, but he felt an undeniable tug of embarrassment.

"I, ah, guess they don't believe in whetting the audience's appetite."

Althea tilted her head, studying the screen with a clinical detachment. It wasn't lovemaking. It wasn't even sex, according to her definition. It was straight porn, more pathetic than titillating.

"I've seen hotter stuff at bachelor parties."

Colt took his eyes from the screen long enough to arch a brow at her. "Oh, really?"

"Tape's surprisingly good quality. And the camera work, if you can call it that, seems pretty professional." She listened to the moans. "Sound, too." She nodded as the camera pulled back for a long shot. "Not the penthouse."

"Must be the place in the mountains. High-class rustic, from the paneling. Bed looks like a Chippendale."

"How do you know?"

"My mother's big on antiques. Look at the lamp by the bed. It's Tiffany, or a damn fine imitation. Ah, the plot thickens...."

They both watched as another woman walked into the frame. A few lines of dialogue indicated that she had come upon her lover and her best friend. The confrontation turned violent.

"I don't think that's fake blood." Althea hissed through her teeth as the first woman took a hard blow to the face. "And I don't think she was expecting that punch."

Colt swore softly as the rest of the scene unfolded. The mixture of sex and violence—violence that was focused on the women—made an ugly picture. He had to clench his fists to keep himself from slamming the television off.

It was no longer a matter of amused embarrassment. It was a matter of revulsion.

"You handling this, Nightshade?" Althea laid a hand on his arm. They both knew what he feared most—that Liz would come on-screen.

"I don't guess I'll be wanting any popcorn."

Instinctively Althea left her hand where it was and moved closer.

There was a plot of sorts, and she began to follow it. A weekend at a ski chalet, two couples who mixed and mingled in several ways. She moved beyond that, picking up the details. The furnishings. Colt had been right—they were first-class. Different camera angles showed that it was a two-story with an open loft and high beamed ceilings. Stone fireplace, hot tub.

In a few artistic shots, she saw that it was snowing lightly. She caught glimpses of screening trees and snow-capped peaks. In one outdoor scene that must have been more than uncomfortable for the actors, she noted that there was no other house or structure close by.

The tape ended without credits. And without Liz. Colt didn't know whether he was relieved or not.

"I don't think it's got much of a shot in the Oscar race." Althea kept her voice light as she rewound the tape. "You okay?"

He wasn't okay. There was a burning in his gut that needed some sort of release. "They were rough on the women," he said carefully. "Really vicious."

"Offhand, I'd say the main customers for this kind of thing would be guys who fantasize about dominance—physical and emotional."

"I don't think you can apply the word fantasy in conjunction with something like this."

"Not all fantasies are pretty," she murmured, thinking. "You know, the quality was good, but some of the acting—and I use the term loosely—was downright pitiful. Could be they let some of their clients live out those fantasies on film."

"Lovely." He took one careful, cleansing breath. "Jade's letter mentioned that she thought one of the girls had been killed. Looks like she might have been right."

"Sadism's a peculiar sexual tool—and one that can often get out of hand. We might be able to make the general area from the outside shots."

She started to eject the tape, but he whirled her around. "How can you be so damn clinical? Didn't that get to you? Doesn't anything?"

"Whatever does, I deal with it. Let's leave personalities out of this."

"No. It goes back to knowing who you're working with. We're talking about the fact that some girl might have been killed for the camera." There was a fury in him that he couldn't control, and a terrible need to vent it. "We've just seen two women slapped, shoved, punched, and threatened with worse. I want to know what watching that did to you."

"It made me sick," she snapped back, jerking away. "And it made me angry. And if I'd let myself, it would have made me sad. But all that matters, all that really matters, is that we have our first piece of hard evidence." She snatched out the tape and replaced it in its bag. "Now, if you want to do me a favor, you'll drop me back at the precinct so that I can turn this over. Then you can give me some space."

"Sure, Lieutenant." He strode to the door to yank it open. "I'll give you all the space you need."

Chapter 5

Colt was holding three ladies. And he thought it was really too bad that the lady he wanted was sitting across the table from him, upping his bet.

"There's your twenty-five, Nightshade, and twenty-five more." Althea tossed chips into the kitty. She held her cards close to her vest, like her thoughts.

"Ah, well…" Sweeney heaved a sigh and studied the trash in his hand as if wishing alone might turn it to gold. "Too rich for my blood."

From her seat between Sweeney and a forensic pathologist named Louie, Cilla considered her pair of fives. "What do you think, Deadeye?"

Keenan, dressed for bed in a Denver Nuggets jersey, bounced on her lap. "Throw the money in."

"Easy for you to say." But her chips clattered onto the pile.

After a personal debate that included a great deal of muttering, shifting and head shaking, Louie tossed in his chips, as well.

"I'll see your twenty-five," Colt drawled. He kept his cigar clamped between his teeth as he counted out chips. "And bump it again."

Boyd just grinned, pleased that he'd folded after the draw. The bet made the rounds again, with only Althea, Cilla and Colt remaining in.

"Three pretty queens," he announced, and laid down his cards.

Althea's eyes glinted when they met his. "Nice. But we don't have room for them in my full house." She spread her cards, revealing three eights and a pair of deuces.

"That puts my two fives to shame." Cilla sighed as Althea raked in the pot. "Okay, kid, you cost me seventy-five cents. Now you have to die." She hauled a giggling Keenan up as she rose.

"Daddy!" He spread his arms and grinned. "Help me! Don't let her do it!"

"Sorry, son." Boyd ruffled Keenan's hair and

gave him a solemn kiss. "Looks like you're doomed. We're going to miss you around here."

Always ready to prolong the inevitable, Keenan hooked his arms around Colt's neck. "Save me!"

Colt kissed the waiting lips and shook his head. "Only one thing in this world scares me, partner, and that's a mama. You're on your own."

Levering in Cilla's arms, the boy made the rounds of the table. When he got to Althea, his eyes gleamed. "Okay? Can I?"

It was an old game, one she was willing to play. "For a nickel."

"I can owe you."

"You already owe me eight thousand dollars and fifteen cents."

"I get my allowance Friday."

"Okay, then." She took him onto her lap for a hug, and he sniffed her hair like a puppy. Colt saw her face soften, watched her hand slide up to stroke the tender nape of the boy's neck.

"It's good," Keenan announced, taking one last exaggerated sniff.

"Don't forget that eight thousand on Friday. Now beat it." After a kiss, she passed him back to Cilla.

"Deal me out," Cilla suggested, and, settling her son on her hip, she carried him upstairs to bed.

"A boy who can talk his way into a woman's lap's a boy to be proud of." Sweeney grinned as he gathered the cards. "My deal. Ante up."

During the next hour, Althea's pile of chips grew slowly, steadily. She enjoyed the monthly poker games that had become a routine shortly after Cilla and Boyd were married. The basic challenge of outwitting her opponents relaxed her almost as much as the domestic atmosphere that had seeped into every corner of the Fletcher home.

She was a cautious player, one who gambled only when satisfied with the odds, and who bet meticulously, thoughtfully, even then. She noted that Colt's pile multiplied, as well, but in fits and starts. He wasn't reckless, she decided. *Ruthless* was the word. Often he bumped the pot when he had nothing, or sat back and let others do the raising when he had a handful of gold.

No pattern, she mused, which she supposed was a pattern of its own.

After Sweeney won a piddling pot with a heart flush, she pushed back from the table. "Anybody want a beer?"

Everybody did. Althea strolled into the kitchen and began to pop tops. She was pouring herself a glass of wine when Colt walked in.

"Thought you could use some help."

"I can handle it."

"I don't figure there's much you can't handle." Damn, the woman was prickly, he thought. "I just thought I'd lend a hand."

Maria had prepared enough sandwiches to satisfy a hungry platoon on a long march. For lack of anything better to do Colt shifted some from platter to plate. He had to get it out, he decided. Now that they were alone and he had the opportunity, he wasn't sure how to start.

"I've got something to say about this afternoon."

"Oh?" Her tone frosty, Althea turned to the refrigerator and took out a bowl of Maria's incomparable guacamole dip.

"I'm sorry."

And nearly dropped it. "Excuse me?"

"Damn it, I'm sorry. Okay?" He hated to apologize—it meant he had made a mistake, one that mattered. "Watching that tape got to me. It made me want to smash something, someone. The closest I could come to it was ripping into you."

Because it was the last thing she would have expected, she was caught off guard. She stood with the bowl in her hand, unsure of her next move. "All right."

"I was afraid I'd see Liz," he continued, compelled to say it all. "I was afraid I wouldn't." At a loss, he picked up one of the opened beers and took a long swallow. "I'm not used to being scared like this."

There was very little he could have said, and nothing he could have done, that would have gotten through her defenses more thoroughly. Touched, and shaken, she set the bowl on the counter and opened a bag of chips.

"I know. It got to me, too. It's not supposed to, but it did." She poured the chips into the bowl, wishing there was something else she could do. Anything else. "I'm sorry things aren't moving faster, Colt."

"They haven't been standing still, either. And I've got you to thank for most of that." He lifted a hand, then dropped it. "Thea, there was something else I wanted to do this afternoon besides punching somebody. I wanted to hold you." He saw the wariness flash into her eyes, quick as a heartbeat, and had to grind down his temper. "Not jump you, Thea. Hold you. There's a difference."

"Yes, there is." She let out a long, quiet breath. There was need in his eyes. Not desire, just need. The need for contact, for comfort, for compassion.

That she understood. "I guess I could have used it, too."

"I still could." It cost him to make the first move, this sort of move. But he stepped toward her and held out his arms.

It cost her, as well, to respond, to move into his arms and encircle him with her own.

And when they were close, when her cheek was resting against his shoulder and his against her hair, they both sighed. The tension drained away like water through a broken dam.

He didn't understand it, wasn't sure he could accept it, but he realized it felt right. Very simply right. Unlike the first time he'd held her, there was no punch of lust, no molten fire in his blood. But there was a warmth, sweet and spreading and solid.

He could have held her like that, just like that, for hours.

She didn't often let herself relax so completely, not with a man, and certainly not with a man who attracted her. But this was so easy, so natural. The steady thudding of his heart lulled her. She nearly nuzzled. The urge was there—to rub her cheek against him, to close her eyes and purr. When she felt him sniffing her hair, she laughed.

"The kid's right," he murmured. "It's good."

"That's going to cost you a nickel, Nightshade."

"Put it on my tab," he told her as she lifted her head to smile at him.

Was it because she'd never looked at him quite that way that it hit him so hard? He couldn't be sure. All he knew was that she was outrageously beautiful, her hair loose and tumbling into his hands, glinting like flame in the hard kitchen light. Her eyes were smiling, deep and tawny and warm with humor. And her mouth—unpainted, curved, slightly parted. Irresistible.

He tilted his head, lowered it, waiting for her to stiffen or draw back. She did neither. Though the humor in her eyes had turned to awareness, the warmth remained. So he touched his lips to hers, gently testing, an experiment in emotions. With their eyes open, they watched each other, as if each were waiting for the other to move back, or leap forward.

When she remained pliant in his arms, he changed the angle, nipping lightly. He felt her tremble, only once, as her eyes darkened, clouded. But they remained open and on his.

She wanted to see him. Needed to. She was afraid that if she closed her eyes she might fall into whatever pit it was that yawned before her. She had to see who he was, to try to understand what there was about this one man that made him capable of turning her system to mush.

No one had done so before. And she'd been proud of her ability to resist, or to control, and smugly amused by men and women who fell under the spell of another. In falling they had suffered the torments of love. She had never been certain the joys balanced those torments.

But as he deepened the kiss, slowly, persuasively deepened it so that not only her lips, but also her mind, her heart, her body, were involved in that contact, she wondered what she had missed by never allowing surrender to mix with power.

"Althea…" He whispered her name as he again, teasingly, changed the angle of the kiss. "Come with me…."

She understood what he was asking. He wanted her to let go, to tumble with him wherever the moment took them. To yield to him, even as he yielded to her.

To gamble, when she wasn't sure of the odds.

He closed his eyes first. The soft, drowsy warmth slid seamlessly into a numbing ache, an ache that was all pleasure. Her eyes fluttered closed on a sigh.

"Hey! How about those beers— Oops!" Boyd winced and struggled not to grin. He slipped his hands into his pockets, and had to prevent himself from whistling a tune as his old friend and his former partner jumped apart like thieves caught in a bust.

"Sorry, guys." He strolled over to gather up the beer bottles himself. It occurred to him that in all the years he'd known Althea, he'd never seen that bemused, punch-drunk look on her face. "Must be something about this kitchen," he added as he headed for the door. "Can't tell you how many times I've found myself occupied the same way in here."

The door swung shut behind him. Althea blew out a long breath.

"Oh, boy" was the best she could manage.

Colt laid a hand on her shoulder. Not for balance, he assured himself, though his legs were weak. Just to keep things nice and light. "He looked pretty damned pleased with himself didn't he?"

"He'll razz me about this," she muttered. "And he'll tell Cilla, so she can razz me, too."

"They've probably got better things to do."

"They're married," she shot back. "Married people love talking about other people's—"

"Other people's what?"

"Stuff."

The more unraveled she became, the more Colt liked it. He was positive that only a privileged few had ever seen the cool lieutenant flustered. He wanted to savor every moment of the experience. Grinning, he leaned back against the counter.

"So? If you really want to drive them crazy, you could let me come home with you tonight."

"In your dreams, Nightshade."

He lifted a brow. Her voice hadn't been quite steady. He liked that—a whole lot. "Well, there's truth in that, darling. Might as well be straight and tell you I'm not willing to wait much longer to turn that dream into reality."

She needed to calm down, needed to do something with her hands. Killing two birds with one stone, she picked up her wine and sipped. "Is that a threat?"

"Althea." There was a world of patience in his voice. That amused him. He couldn't recall ever having been patient about anything before. "We both know what just went on here can't be turned into a threat. It was nice." He flicked a finger down her hair. "If we'd been alone somewhere, it would have turned out a lot nicer." The intent flickered in his eyes too quickly for her to avoid the result. His hand fisted in her hair, held her still. "I want you, Althea, and I want you bad. You can make out of that whatever you choose."

She felt a skip of something sprint down her spine. It wasn't fear. She'd been a cop long enough to recognize fear in all its forms. And she'd lived her life her own way long enough to remain cautious. "It seems to me that you want a great many things. You want Liz back, you want the men responsible for keeping her from her parents caught and punished. You want to do those things your way, with my cooperation. And—" she sipped her wine again, her eyes cool and level "—you want to go to bed with me."

She was amazing, Colt reflected. She had to be feeling some portion of the need and the desperation he was experiencing. Yet she might have been discussing a change in the weather. "That about sums it up. Why don't you tell me what you want?"

She was afraid she knew exactly what she wanted, and it was standing almost close enough to taste. "The difference between you and me, Nightshade, is that I know you don't always get what you want. Now I'm going to pack it in. I've had a long day. You can check with me tomorrow.

We'll have the sketches from Meena. Something might turn up when we run them."

"All right." He'd let her go—for now, he thought. The trouble with a woman like Althea, he mused, was that a man would always be tempted to seduce her, and he would always crave her coming to him freely.

"Thea?"

She paused at the kitchen door, looked back. "Yes?"

"What are we going to do about this?"

She felt a sigh building—not one of weariness, one of longing—and choked it off. "I don't know," she said, as truthfully as she could. "I wish I did."

By nine-thirty the following morning, Colt was cooling his heels in Althea's office. There wasn't much room in her cubbyhole to cool anything. Out of sheer boredom, he flipped through some of the papers on her desk. Reports, he noted, in that peculiar language cops used, a language that was both concise and florid. Vehicles proceeded in a southwesterly direction, alleged perpetrators created disturbances, arresting officers apprehended suspects after responding to 312s and 515s.

She wrote a damn good report, if you were into

such bureaucratic hogwash. Which, he decided, she obviously was. Rules-and-Regulations Grayson, he thought, and closed the file. Maybe his biggest problem was that he'd seen that there was a lot more to her than the straight-arrow cop.

He'd seen her hold a gun, steady as a rock, while her eyes were alive with fear and determination. He'd felt her respond like glory to an impulsive and urgent embrace. He'd watched her cuddle a child, soften with compassion and freeze like a hailstone.

He'd seen too much, and he knew he hadn't seen nearly enough.

Liz was his priority, had to be. Yet Althea remained lodged inside him, like a bullet in the flesh. Hot, painful, and impossible to ignore.

It made him angry. It made him itchy. And when she swept into the room, it made him snarl.

"I've been waiting for the best part of a damn hour. I haven't got time for this."

"That's a shame." She dropped another file onto her desk, noting immediately that her papers had been disturbed. "Could be you're watching too much TV, Nightshade. That's the only place a cop gets to work on one case at a time."

"I'm not a cop."

"That's more than obvious. And next time you have to wait for me, keep your nose out of my papers."

"Listen, Lieutenant—" He broke off, swearing, when her phone rang.

"Grayson." She slipped into her chair as she spoke, her hand already reaching for a pencil. "Yeah. Yeah, I got it. That was quick work, Sergeant. I appreciate it. I'll be sure to do that if I get over your way. Thanks again." She broke the connection and immediately began to dial again. "Kansas City located Jade's mother," she told Colt. "She'd moved from the Kansas side to Missouri."

"Is Jade with her?"

"That's what I'm going to try to find out." As she completed the call, Althea checked her watch. "She waits tables at night. Odds are I'll catch her at home at this hour."

Before Colt could speak again, Althea shot up a hand for silence.

"Hello, I'd like to speak with Janice Willowby." A sleepy and obviously irritated voice informed her that Janice didn't live there. "Is this Mrs. Willowby? Mrs. Willowby, this is Lieutenant Grayson, Denver Police— No, ma'am, she hasn't done anything. She isn't in any trouble. We believe she might be of some help to us on a case. Have you heard from your daughter in the last few weeks?" She listened patiently as the woman denied having been in contact with Janice and irritably demanded information. "Mrs. Willowby, Janice isn't a fugitive from justice, or under any sort of suspicion. However, we are anxious to contact her." Her eyes hardened, quickly, coldly. "Excuse me? Since I'm not asking you to turn your daughter in, I don't see a reward as being applicable. If—"

Colt thrust a hand over the receiver. "Five thousand," he stated. "If she gets us Jade, and Jade leads us to Liz." He saw the spitting denial in her eyes, but held firm. "It's not up to you. The reward's private."

Althea sucked in her disgust. "Mrs. Willowby, there is a private party authorizing the sum of five thousand for information on Janice, on the condition that this then results in the satisfactory close of the investigation. Yes, I'm quite sure you can have it in cash. Oh, yes, I'm sure you will see what you can do. You can reach me twenty-four hours a day, at this number." She repeated it twice. "Collect, of course. That's Lieutenant Althea Grayson, Denver. I hope you do."

After hanging up the phone, she sat simmering. "It's no wonder girls like Jade take off and end up

on the streets. She didn't give a damn about her
daughter, just wanted to be sure no backlash was
going to come her way. If Jade had been in any
trouble, she'd have been willing to trade her for
cash in the blink of an eye."

"Not everybody has the maternal instincts of
Donna Reed."

"You're telling me." Because emotions would
interfere with the job at hand, Althea shelved them.
"Meena's been working with the police artist, and
she's come up with some pretty good likenesses.
One of them matches one of the stars from the
production we watched yesterday."

"Which one?"

"The guy in the red leather G-string. We're running a make through Vice to start. It'll take time."

"I don't have time."

She set aside the pencil, folded her hands. She
wouldn't lose her temper, she promised herself.
Not again. "Do you have a better way?"

"No." He turned away, then swung back. "Any
prints on the car used to hit Billings?"

"Clean."

"The penthouse?"

"No prints. Some hair fibers. They won't help
us catch them, but they'll be good for tying it up

in court. The lab's working on the tape, and the note. We could get lucky."

"How about missing persons? A Jane Doe at the morgue? Jade said she thought one of the girls was killed."

"Nothing's turned up. If they did kill someone, and she'd been in the life for a while, a missing-persons report's unlikely. I've checked all the unidentified and suspicious deaths over the last three months. Nobody fits the profile."

"Any luck in the homeless shelters, runaway hostels, halfway houses?"

"Not yet." She hesitated, then decided it was best that they talk it through. "There's something I've been kicking around."

"Go ahead, kick it my way."

"We've got a couple of baby faces on the force. Good cops. We can put them undercover, out on the street. See if they get a movie offer."

Colt rolled it around in his head. That, too, would take time, he mused. But at least it was a chance. "It's a tricky spot. Do you have anyone good enough to handle it?"

"I said I did. I'd do it myself—"

"No." His abrupt denial was like the lash of a whip.

Althea inclined her head and continued without a flinch. "I said, I'd do it myself, but I can't pass for a teenager. Apparently our producer prefers kids. I'll set it in motion."

"Okay. Can you get me a dupe of the tape?"

She smiled. "Evenings too dull for you?"

"Very funny. Can you?"

She thought it through. It wasn't strictly procedure, but it couldn't do any harm. "I'll check with the lab. Meanwhile, I'm going to roust the bartender at Clancy's. I'm betting he's the one who tipped off the bunch on Second Avenue. We might sweat something out of him."

"I'll go with you."

She shook her head. "I'm taking Sweeney." She smiled, fully, easily. "A big Irish cop, a bar called Clancy's. It just seems to fit."

"He's a lousy poker player."

"Yeah, but a darlin' man," she said, surprising him by slipping into a perfect Irish brogue.

"How about I go along anyway?"

"How about you wait for me to call you?" She rose, pulled a navy blazer from the back of her chair. She wore pleated slacks of the same color and texture and a paler blue blouse in a silky material. Her shoulder harness and weapon looked so natural on her, they might have been fashion accessories.

"You will call me."

"I said I would."

Because it seemed right, he laid his hands on her shoulders, and briefly rested his brow on hers. "Marleen called me this morning. I don't like to think I was giving her false hope, but I told her we were getting closer. I had to tell her that."

"Whatever eases her mind is the right thing to say." She couldn't help it. She pressed a hand briefly to his cheek in comfort, then let it drop. "Hang tough, Nightshade. We've gathered a lot of information in a short amount of time."

"Yeah." He lifted his head and slid his hands down her arms until he could link fingers with her. "I'll let you go find your intimidating Irishman. But there's one more thing." He raised their linked hands, studying the contrast of texture, tone and size. "Sooner or later, we'll be going off the clock." His gaze shifted to meet hers. "Then we'll have to deal with other things."

"Then we'll deal with them. But you may not like the way it shakes down."

He caught her chin in one hand, kissed her hard, then released her before she could do more than hiss. "Same goes. You be careful out there, Lieutenant."

"I was born careful, Nightshade." She walked away, shrugging into the blazer as she went.

Ten hours later, she parked her car in her building's garage and headed for the elevator. She was ready for a hot bath pregnant with bubbles, a glass of icy white wine, and some slow blues, heavy on the bass.

As she rode to her floor, she leaned against the back wall and shut her eyes. They hadn't gotten very far with the bartender, Leo Dorsetti. Bribes hadn't worked, and veiled threats hadn't, either. Althea didn't doubt he had connections with the pornography ring. Nor did she doubt that he was worried that the same fate might befall him that had Wild Bill.

So she needed more than a threat. She needed to dig up something on Leo Dorsetti. Something solid enough that she could drag him downtown and into interrogation.

Once she had him, she could crack him. She was damn sure of that.

She jingled her keys as she walked through the open elevator doors and into the hall. Now it was time to put the cop on hold, at least for an hour or two. Obsessing over a case usually equalled making mistakes on a case. So she'd pack it away into a corner of her mind, let it sit, let it ripen, while the woman indulged in a purely selfish evening.

She'd already unlocked the door, pushed it open, when the alarm went off in her head. She didn't question what tripped it, just whipped out her weapon. Automatically she followed standard entry procedure, checking in corners and behind the door.

Her eyes scanned the room, noting that nothing was out of place—unless she counted the Bessie Smith record currently playing on the turntable. And the scent. She took a quick whiff, identifying cooking, something spicy. It made her mouth water in response, even as her mind stayed alert.

A sound from the kitchen had her whirling in that direction, ending in the spread-legged police stance, her weapon steady in both hands.

Colt stopped in the doorway, wiping his hands on a dishcloth. Smiling, he leaned back against the jamb. "Hi there, darling. And how was your day?"

Chapter 6

Althea lowered her gun. She didn't raise her voice. The words she chose, quiet and precise, made her feelings known with more clarity than a shout could have.

When she'd finished, Colt could only shake his head in admiration. "I don't believe I've ever been cussed out with more style. Now, I'd be obliged if you'd holster that gun. Not that I figure you'd use it and risk getting blood all over your floor."

"It might be worth it." She slapped her gun back in place, but her eyes never left his. "You have the right to remain silent...." she began.

Wisely, Colt stifled a chuckle. He held up a hand. "What're you doing?"

"I'm reading you your rights before I haul your butt in for nighttime breaking and entering."

He didn't doubt she'd do it. She'd have him booked, fingerprinted and photographed without breaking stride. "I'll waive them, providing you listen to an explanation."

"It better be good." Shrugging out of her blazer, she tossed it over the back of the chair. "How did you get in here?"

"I, ah… Through the door?"

Her eyes narrowed. "You have the right to an attorney."

Obviously humor wasn't going to do the trick. "Okay, I'm busted." He tossed up both hands in a gesture of surrender. "I picked the lock. It's a damn good one, too. Or maybe I'm getting rusty."

"You picked the lock." She nodded, as if it were no more than she'd expected. "You carry a concealed weapon—an ASP nine-millimeter…"

"Good eye, Lieutenant."

"And a knife that likely exceeds the legal limit," she continued. "Now it appears you also carry lock picks."

"They come in handy." And it was something he

preferred not to dwell on when she was in this sort of mood. "Now, I figured you had a rough day, and you deserved coming home to a hot meal and some cold wine. I also figured you'd be a little testy coming in and finding me here. But I have to believe you'll come around after you've had a taste of my linguine."

Maybe, she thought, maybe if she closed her eyes for a minute, it would all go away. But when she tried it, he was still there, grinning at her. "Your linguine?"

"Linguine marinara. I'd claim it was my sainted mother's recipe, but she never boiled an egg in her life. How about that wine?"

"Sure. Why the hell not?"

"That's the way." He stepped back into the kitchen. Deciding she could always kill him later, Althea followed. The aromas drifting through the air were heaven. "You like white," he said as he poured two glasses, using her best crystal. "This is a nice, full-bodied Italian that won't embarrass my sauce. Bold, but classy. See if it suits you."

She accepted the glass, allowed him to clink his against hers, then sipped. The wine tasted like liquid heaven. "Who the hell are you, Nightshade?"

"Why, I'm the answer to your prayers. Why don't we go in and sit down? You know you want to take your shoes off."

She did, but she obstinately kept them on as she walked back and lowered herself onto the couch. "Explain."

"I just did."

"If you cannot afford an attorney—"

"God, you're tough." He let out a long breath and stretched out beside her. "Okay, I have a couple of reasons. One, I know you've been putting in a lot of extra time on my business…."

"It's my—"

"Job?" he finished for her. "Maybe. But I know when someone's taking those extra steps, the kind that eat into personal time, and fixing you dinner's just a way of saying thanks."

It was a damn nice gesture, too, she thought, though she wasn't willing to say so. Yet. "You might have mentioned the idea to me earlier."

"It was an impulse. You ever have them?"

"Don't push your luck, Nightshade."

"Right. Well, to get back to the whys. There's also the fact that I haven't been able to snatch more than an hour at a time to clear this whole mess out of my head. Cooking helps me recharge. Maria wasn't likely to turn her stove over to me, so I thought of you." He reached out to curl a lock of her hair around his finger. "I think of you a lot. And finally, and simply, I wanted the evening with you."

He was getting to her. Althea wanted to believe that it was the glorious scents sneaking out of the kitchen that were weakening her. But she didn't believe it. "So you broke into my home and invaded my privacy."

"The only thing I poked into was your kitchen cupboards. It was tempting," he admitted, "but I didn't go any farther than that."

Frowning, Althea swirled the wine in her glass. "I don't like your methods, Nightshade. But I think I'm going to like your linguine."

She didn't like it. She adored it. It was difficult to harbor resentments when her palate was being so thoroughly seduced. She'd had men cook for her before, but she couldn't remember ever being so completely charmed.

Here was Colt Nightshade, very possibly armed to the teeth beneath his faded jeans and chambray shirt, serving her pasta by candlelight. Not that it was romantic, she thought. She was too smart to fall for any conventional trappings. But it was funny, and oddly sweet.

By the time she'd worked her way through one helping and was starting on a second, she'd filled him in on her progress. The lab reports were expected within twenty-four hours, the bartender at Clancy's was under surveillance, and an undercover officer was being prepped to hit the streets.

Colt filed her information away and traded it for some of his own. He'd talked to some of the local working girls that afternoon. Whether due to his charm or to the money that had changed hands, he'd learned that a girl who went by the street name Lacy hadn't been seen in any of her usual haunts for the past several weeks.

"She fits the profile," he continued, topping off Althea's wineglass. "Young, tiny. Girls said she was a brunette, but liked to wear a blond wig."

"Did she have a pimp?"

"Uh-uh. Free-lancer. I went by the rooms she'd been renting." Colt broke a piece of garlic bread in two and passed Althea half. "Talked to the landlord—a prince of a guy. Since she'd missed a couple of weekly rent payments, he'd packed up her stuff. Pawned what was worth anything, trashed the rest."

"I'll see if anybody at Vice knows about her."

"Good. I hit some of the shelters again," he went on. "The halfway houses, showing Liz's picture around, and the police sketches." He frowned, toying with the rest of his meal. "I couldn't get anyone to ID. Had a hard enough time convincing any of the kids that they should look at the pictures. Most of the kids want to act tough, invincible, and all you see is the confusion in their eyes."

"When you're dealing with that kind of confusion, you have to be tough. Most of them come from homes that are torn apart by drugs, drinking, physical and sexual abuse. Or they got into substance abuse all on their own and don't know how to get out again." She moved her shoulders. "Either way, running seems like the best way out."

"It wasn't like that for Liz."

"No," she agreed. It was time for him to turn it off, as well, she decided. If only for a few minutes. She scraped a last bite from her plate. "You know, Nightshade, you could give up playing the adventurer and go into catering. You'd make a fortune."

He understood what she was doing, and he put some effort into accommodating her. "I prefer small, private parties."

Her gaze flicked up to his, then back to her glass. "So, if it wasn't your sainted mother who taught you to make world-class linguine, who did?"

"We had this terrific Irish cook when I was growing up. Mrs. O'Malley."

"An Irish cook who taught you Italian cuisine."

"She could make anything—from lamb stew to coq au vin. 'Colt, me boy,' she used to tell me, 'the best thing a man can do for himself is to learn to feed himself well. Depending on a woman to fill your belly's a mistake.'" The memory made him grin. "When I'd gotten into trouble, which was most of the time, she'd sit me down in the kitchen. I'd get lectures on behavior, and the proper way to debone a chicken."

"Quite a combination."

"The stuff on behavior didn't stick." He toasted her. "But I make a hell of a chicken pot pie. And when Mrs. O'Malley retired—oh, almost ten years ago now—my mother went into a dark state of depression."

Althea's lips curved on the rim of her glass. "And hired another cook."

"A French guy with a bad attitude. She loves him."

"A French chef in Wyoming."

"I live in Wyoming," he said. "They live in Houston. We get along better that way. What about your family? Are they from around here?"

"I don't have one. What about your law degree? Why haven't you done anything with it?"

"I didn't say I hadn't." He studied her for a moment. She'd certainly dropped his question like a hot coal. It was something he'd have to come back to. "I found out I wasn't suited to spending hours hunched over law books, trying to outwit justice on technicalities."

"So you went into the air force."

"It was a good way to learn how to fly."

"But you're not a pilot."

"Sometimes I am." He smiled. "Sorry, Thea, I don't fit into a slot. I've got enough money that I can do what suits me when it suits me."

That wasn't good enough. "And the military didn't suit you?"

"For a while it did. Then I had enough." He shrugged and sat back. The candlelight flickered on his face and in his eyes. "I learned some things. Just like I learned from Mrs. O'Malley, and from prep school, from Harvard, and from this old Indian horse trainer I met in Tulsa some years back. You never know when you're going to use what you've learned."

"Who taught you to pick locks?"

"You're not going to hold that against me, are you?" He leaned forward to flick a finger over her hair, and to pour more wine. "I picked it up in the service. I was in what you might call a special detachment."

"Covert operations," she said, translating. It was no surprise. "That's why so much of your record's classified."

"It's old news, should be declassified by now. But that's the way of it, isn't it? Bureaucrats like secrets almost as much as they like red tape. What I did was gather information, or plant information, maybe defuse certain volatile situations, or stir them up, depending on the orders." He drank again. "I guess we could say I started doing favors for people—only these people ran the government." His lip curled. "Or tried to."

"You don't like the system, do you?"

"I like what works." For an instant only, his eyes darkened. "I saw plenty that didn't work. So…" He shrugged, and the mood was gone. "I got out, bought myself a few horses and cows, played rancher. Looks like old habits die hard, because now I do favors for people again. Only now I have to like them first."

"Some people might say that you've had a hard time deciding what you want to do when you grow up."

"Some people might. I figure I've been doing it. What about you? What's the back story on Althea Grayson?"

"It's nothing that would sell to the movies." Relaxed, she rested her elbows on the table, running a finger around the rim of her glass until the crystal sang. "I went straight into the academy when I was eighteen. No detours."

"Why?"

"Why a cop?" She mulled over her answer. "Because I do like the system. It's not perfect, but if you keep at it, you can make it work. And the law…there are people out there who want to make it work. Too many lives get lost in the cracks. It means something when you can pull one out."

"I can't argue with that." Without thinking about it, he laid a hand over hers. "I could always see that Boyd was meant to make law and order work. Until recently, he was about the only cop I respected enough to trust."

"I think you just gave me a compliment."

"You can be sure of it. The two of you have a lot in common. A clear-sightedness, a stubborn kind of valor, a steady compassion." He smiled, toying with her fingers. "The kid we got off the roof—I went to see her, too. She had a lot to say about the pretty lady with the red hair who brought her a baby doll."

"So I did a follow-up. It's my job to—"

"Bull." Delighted with her response, he picked up her hand, kissed it. "It had nothing to do with duty, and everything to do with you. Having a soft side doesn't make you less of a cop, Thea. It just makes you a kinder one."

She knew where this was leading, but she didn't pull her hand away. "Just because I have a soft spot for kids doesn't mean I've got one for you."

"But you do," he murmured. "I get to you." Watching her, he skimmed his lips down to her wrist. The pulse there beat steady, but it also beat fast. "I'm going to keep getting to you."

"Maybe you do." She was too smart to continue to deny the obvious. "That doesn't mean anything's going to come of it. I don't sleep with every man who attracts me."

"I'm glad to hear it. Then again, you're going to do a lot more than sleep with me." He chuckled and kissed her hand again. "God, I love it when you smirk, Thea. It drives me crazy. What I was going to say was, when we get each other to bed, sleeping's not going to be a priority. So maybe you should catch some shut-eye." He rose, pulling her to her feet. "Kiss me good-night, and I'll let you get some now."

The surprise in her eyes made him grin again. He'd wait until later to pat himself on the back for his strategy.

"You thought I cooked you dinner and kept you company so I could use it as a springboard to seduction." On a windy sigh, he shook his head. "Althea, I'm wounded. Close to crushed."

She laughed, keeping a friendly hand in his. "You know, Nightshade, sometimes I almost like you. Almost."

"See, that's just a couple of short steps away from you being nuts about me." He gathered her close, and the instant twisting in his gut mocked his light tone. "If I'd bothered to make dessert, you'd be begging for me."

Amused, she tucked her tongue in her cheek. "Your loss. Everybody knows cannoli turns me into a wild woman."

"I'll sure as hell remember that." He kissed her lightly, watched her smile. And felt his heart turn over. "There must be a bakery around here where I can pick up some Italian pastries."

"Nope. You missed your shot." She brought a hand to his chest, telling herself she was going to end the interlude now, while she could still feel her legs under her. "Thanks for the pasta."

"Sure." But he continued to stare down at her, his eyes sharpening, focusing, as if he were struggling to see past the ivory skin, the delicate bones. Something was happening here, he realized. Something internal that he couldn't quite get a grip on. "You have something in your eyes."

Her nerves were dancing. "What?"

"I don't know." He spoke slowly, as if measuring each word. "Sometimes I can almost see it. When I do, it makes me wonder where you've been. Where we're going."

Her lungs were backing up. She took a careful breath to clear them. "*You* were going home."

"Yeah. In a minute. Too easy to tell you you're beautiful," he murmured, as if speaking to himself. "You hear that too much, and it's too superficial to carry any weight with you. It should be enough for me, but there's something else in there. I keep coming back to it." Still seeking, he drew her closer. "What is it about you, Althea? What is it I can't shake loose?"

"There's nothing. You're too used to looking for shadows."

"No, you've got them." Slowly he slid a hand up to cup her cheek. "And what I have is a problem."

"What problem?"

"Try this."

He lowered his mouth to hers and had every muscle in her body going lax. It wasn't demanding, it wasn't urgent. It was devastating. The kiss tumbled her deeper, deeper, bombarding her with emotions she had no defense against. His feelings were free and ripe and poured over her, into her, so that she was covered and filled and surrounded by them.

No escape, she thought, and heard her own muffled sound of despair with a dull acceptance. He'd breached a defense she had taken for granted, one she might never fully shore up again.

She could tell herself again and again that she wouldn't fall in love, that she couldn't fall in love with a man she hardly knew. But her heart was already laughing at logic.

He felt her give—not all the way, not yet, but

give yet another degree of self. There was more than heat here, though, sweet heaven, there was heat. But there was a kind of discovery, as well. For Colt, it was a revelation to discover that one woman—this woman—could tangle up his mind, rip open his heart, and leave him helpless.

"I'm losing ground here." He kept his hands firm on her shoulders as he pulled back. "I'm losing it fast."

"It's too much." It was a poor response, but the best she could summon.

"You're telling me." There was tension in her shoulders again, and in his. It compelled him to step away. "I've never felt like this before. And that's no line," he said when she turned away from him.

"I know. I wish it were." She gripped the back of the chair, where her shoulder holster hung. A symbol of duty, she thought. Of control, of what she had made of herself. "Colt, I think we're both getting in deeper than we might like."

"Maybe we've been treading water long enough."

She was very much afraid that she was ready, willing, even eager, to sink. "I don't let personal business interfere with my job. If we can't keep this under control, you should consider working with someone else."

"We've been working together just fine," he said between his teeth. "Don't pull out any lame excuses because you don't want to face up to what's going on between us."

"It's the best I've got." Her knuckles had turned white on the chair. "And it's not an excuse, only a reason. You want me to say you scare me. All right. You scare me. This scares me. And I don't think you want a partner who can't focus because you make her nervous."

"Maybe I'm happier with that than with one who's so focused it's hard to tell if she's human." She wasn't going to pull away from him now. He'd be damned if he'd let her. "Don't tell me you can't work on two levels, Thea, or that you can't function as a cop when you've got a problem in your personal life."

"Maybe I just don't want to work with you."

"That's tough. You're stuck. If you want to put this on hold, I'll try to oblige you. But you're not backing off from Liz because you're afraid to let yourself feel something for me."

"I'm thinking about Liz, and what's best for her."

"How the hell would you know?" he exploded,

and if it was unreasonable, he didn't give a damn. He was on the edge of falling in love with a woman who was calmly telling him she didn't want him in any area of her life. He was desperate to find a frightened girl, and the person who'd helped him make progress toward doing so was threatening to pull out. "How the hell would you know about her or anyone else? You've got yourself so wrapped up in regulations and procedure that you can't feel. No, not can't. Won't. You won't feel. You'll risk your life, but one brush with emotion and up goes the shield. Everything's so tidy for you, isn't it, Althea? There's some poor scared kid out there, but she's just another case for you, just another job."

"*Don't* you tell me how I feel." Her control snapped as she shoved the chair aside, clattering to the floor between them. "Don't tell me what I understand. You can't possibly know what's inside me. Do you think you know Liz, or any of those girls you talked with today? You've walked into shelters and halfway houses, and you think you understand?"

Her eyes glinted, not with tears, but with a rage so sharp he could only stand and let it slice at him. "I know there are plenty of kids who need help, and not always enough help to go around."

"Oh, that's so easy." She strode across the room and back in a rare show of useless motion. "Write a check, pass a bill, make a speech. It's so effortless. You haven't a clue what it's like to be alone, to be afraid or to be caught up in that grinding machine we toss displaced kids into. I spent most of my life in that machine, so don't tell me I don't feel. I know what it's like to want out so bad you run even when there's no place to go. And I know what it's like to be yanked back, to be helpless, to be abused and trapped and miserable. I understand plenty. And I know that Liz has a family who love her, and we'll get her back to them. No matter what, we'll get her back, and she won't be caught in that cycle. So don't you tell me she's just another case, because she matters. They all matter."

She broke off, running a shaky hand through her hair. At the moment, she wasn't sure which was bigger, her embarrassment or her anger. "I'd like you to go now," she said quietly. "I'd really like you to go."

"Sit down." When she didn't respond, he walked over and pressed her into a chair. She was trembling, and the fact that he'd played a part in causing that made him feel as if he'd punched a hole in something precious and fragile. "I'm sorry.

That's a record for me, apologizing to the same person twice in one day." He started to brush a hand over her hair, but stopped himself. "Do you want some water?"

"No. I just want you to leave."

"I can't do it." He lowered himself to the footstool in front of her so that their eyes were level. "Althea..."

She sat back, her eyes shut. She felt as though she'd raced to the top of a mountain and leapt off. "Nightshade, I'm not in the mood to tell you my life story, so if that's what you're waiting for, you know where the door is."

"That'll keep." He took a chance and reached for her hand. It was steady now, he noted, but cold. "Let's try something else. What we've got here are two separate problems. Finding Liz is number one. She's an innocent, a victim, and she needs help. I could find her on my own, but that would take too long. Every day that goes by... Well, too many days have gone by already. I need you to work with me, because you can cut through channels it would take me twice as long to circumvent. And because I trust you to put everything you've got into getting her home."

"All right." She kept her eyes closed, willing the

tension away. "We'll find her. If not tomorrow, the next day. But we'll find her."

"Second problem." He looked down at their hands, studying the way the second hand on her watch ticked off the time. "I think…ah, and since this is a new area for me, I want to qualify it by saying that it's only an opinion…"

"Nightshade." She opened her eyes again, and there was a ghost of a smile in them. "I swear you sound just like a lawyer."

He winced, shifted. "I don't think you should insult a man who's about to tell you he's pretty sure he's in love with you." She jolted. He'd have bet the farm that he could pull a gun and she wouldn't flinch. But mention love and she jumped six inches off the chair. "Don't panic," he continued while she searched for her voice. "I said 'I think.' That leaves us with a safe area to play with."

"Sounds more like a mine field to me." Because she was afraid it might start shaking again, she drew her hand away from his. "I think it would be wise, under the circumstances, to table that for the time being."

"Now who sounds like a lawyer?" He grinned, not at all sure why it seemed so appropriate to laugh at himself. "Darling, you think it puts the fear of God into you? Picture what it does to me. I only brought it up because I'm hoping that'll make it easier to deal with. For all I know, it's just a touch of the flu or something."

"That would be good." She choked back a laugh, terrified it would sound giddy. "Get plenty of rest, drink fluids."

"I'll give that a try." He leaned forward, not displeased to see the wariness in her eyes or the bracing of her shoulders. "But if it's not the flu, or some other bug, I'm going to do something about it. Whatever that might be can wait until we've settled the first problem. Until we do, I won't bring up love, or all the stuff that generally follows along after it—you know, like marriage and family and a two-car garage."

For the first time since he'd known her, he saw her totally at a loss. Her eyes were huge, and her mouth was slack. He would have sworn that if he tapped her, she'd keel over like a sapling in a storm.

"Guess it's just as well I don't, since talking about them in the abstract sense seems to have put you in a coma."

"I…" She managed to close her mouth, swallow, then speak. "I think you've lost your mind."

"Me, too." Lord knew why he felt so cheerful about it. "So for now let's concentrate on digging up those bad guys. Deal?"

"And if I agree, you're not going to sneak in any of that other stuff?"

His smile spread slowly. "Are you willing to take my word on it?"

"No." She steadied herself and smiled back. "But I'm willing to bet I can deflect anything you toss out."

"I'll take that bet." He held out a hand. "Partner." They shook, solemnly. "Now, why don't we—"

The phone interrupted what Althea was sure would have been an unprofessional suggestion. She slipped by Colt and picked up the extension in the kitchen.

It gave him a moment to think about what he'd started. To smile. To think about how he'd like to finish it. Before he'd wound his fantasy up, she was striding back. She righted the chair, snagged her shoulder harness.

"Our friend Leo, the bartender? We just busted him for selling coke out of his back room." The warrior look was back on her face as she shrugged into the harness. "They're bringing him in for interrogation."

"I'm right behind you."

"Behind me is just where you'll stay, Nightshade," she said as she slipped into her blazer. "If Boyd clears it, you can observe through the glass, but that's the best deal you'll get."

He chafed at the restraint. "Let me sit in. I'll keep my mouth shut."

"Don't make me laugh." She grabbed her purse on the way to the door. "Take it or leave it—partner."

He swore at her, and slammed the door behind him. "I'll take it."

Chapter 7

Colt's initial frustration at being stuck behind the two-way glass faded as he watched Althea work. Her patient, detail-by-detail interrogation had a style all its own. It surprised Colt to label that style not only meticulous, but relentless, as well.

She never allowed Leo to draw her off track, never betrayed any reaction to his sarcasm, and never—not even when Leo tried abusive language and veiled threats—raised her voice.

She played poker the same way, he remembered. Coolly, methodically, without a flicker of emotion until it was time to cash in her chips. But

Colt was beginning to see through the aloof shell into the woman behind it.

Certainly he'd been able to surprise many varied emotions from the self-contained lieutenant. Passion, anger, sympathy, even speechless shock. He had a feeling he'd only scratched the surface. There was a wealth of emotions beneath that tidy, professional and undeniably stunning veneer. He intended to keep digging until he unearthed them all.

"Long night." Boyd came up behind him bearing two mugs of steaming coffee.

"I've had longer." Colt accepted the mug, sipped. "This stuff's strong enough to do the tango." He winced and drank again. "Does the captain usually come in for a routine interrogation?"

"The captain does when he has a personal interest." Fletcher watched Althea a moment, noting that she sat, serene and unruffled, as Leo jerkily lit one cigarette from the butt of another. "Is she getting anything?"

With some effort, Colt restrained an urge to beat against the glass just to prove he could do something. "He's still tap dancing."

"He'll wear out long before she does."

"I've already figured that out for myself." They both lapsed into silence as Leo snarled out a par-

ticularly foul insult and Althea responded by asking if he'd like to repeat that statement for the
record. "She doesn't ruffle," Colt commented.
"Fletch, have you ever seen the way a cat'll sit outside a mouse hole?" He flicked a glance at Boyd,
then looked back through the glass. "That cat just
sits there, hardly blinking, maybe for hours. Inside
the hole, the mouse starts to go crazy. He can smell
that cat, see those eyes staring in at him. After a
while, I guess, the mouse circuits in his brain over-
load, and he makes a break for it. The cat just
whips out one paw, and it's over."

Colt sipped more coffee, nodded at the glass.
"That's one gorgeous cat."

"You've gotten to know her pretty well in a
short amount of time."

"Oh, I've got a ways to go yet. All those layers,"
he murmured, almost to himself. "Can't say I've
ever run into a woman who had me just as interested in peeling the layers of her psyche as peeling off her clothes."

The image had Boyd scowling into his coffee.
Althea was a grown woman, he reminded himself,
and more than able to take care of herself. Boyd remembered he'd been amused to find Colt and his
former partner in a clinch in his kitchen. But the

idea of it going further, of his friends leaping into the kind of quick, physical relationship that could leave them both battered at the finish, disturbed him.

Particularly when he thought of Colt's talent with women. It was a talent they both had, and both of them had enjoyed the benefits of that talent over the years. But they weren't discussing just any woman this time. This was Althea.

"You know," Boyd began, feeling his way with the care of a blind man in a maze, "Thea's special. She can handle pretty much anything that comes her way."

"And does," Colt added.

"Yeah, and does. But that's not to say that she doesn't have her vulnerabilities. I wouldn't want to see her hurt. I wouldn't like that at all."

Mildly surprised, Colt lifted a brow. "A warning? Sounds like the same kind you gave me about your sister Natalie about a million years ago."

"Comes to the same thing. Thea's family."

"And you think I could hurt her."

Boyd let out a weary breath. He wasn't enjoying this conversation. "I'm saying, if you did, I'd have to bruise several of your vital organs. I'd be sorry, but I'd have to do it."

Colt acknowledged that with a thoughtful nod. "Who won the last time we went at it?"

Despite his discomfort, Boyd grinned. "I think it was a draw."

"Yeah, that's how I remember it. It was over a woman then, too, wasn't it?"

"Cheryl Anne Madigan." This time Boyd's sigh was nostalgic.

"Little blonde?"

"Nope, tall brunette. Big...blue eyes."

"Right." Colt laughed, shook his head. "I wonder whatever happened to pretty Cheryl Anne."

They fell into a comfortable silence for a moment, reminiscing. Through the speakers they could hear Althea's calm, relentless questioning.

"Althea's a long way from Cheryl Anne Madigan," Colt murmured. "I wouldn't want to hurt her, but I can't promise it won't happen. The thing is, Fletch, for the first time I've run into a woman who matters enough to hurt me back." Colt took another bracing sip. "I think I'm in love with her."

Boyd choked and was forced to set down his mug before he dumped the contents all over his shirt. He waited a beat, tapped a hand against his ear as if to clear it. "You want to say that again? I don't think I caught it."

"You heard me," Colt muttered. Leave it to a friend, he thought, to humiliate you at an emotionally vulnerable moment. "I got almost the same reaction from her when I told her."

"You told her?" Boyd struggled to keep one ear on the interrogation while he absorbed this new and fascinating information. "What did she say?"

"Not much of anything."

The frustration in Colt's voice tickled Boyd so much, he had to bite the tip of his tongue to keep from grinning. "Well, at least she didn't laugh in your face."

"She didn't seem to think it was very funny." Colt blew out a breath and wished Boyd had thought to lace the coffee with a good dose of brandy. "She just sat there, going pale, kind of gaping at me."

"That's a good sign." Boyd patted Colt's shoulder comfortingly. "It's real hard to throw her off that way."

"I figured it was best if it was out, you know? It would give us both time to decide what to do about it." He smiled through the glass at Althea, who continued to sit, cool and unruffled, while Leo gulped down water with a trembling hand. "Though I've pretty much figured out what I'm going to do about it."

"Which is?"

"Well, unless I wake up some morning real soon and realize I've had some sort of brain seizure, I'm going to marry her."

"Marry her?" Boyd rocked back on his heels and chuckled. "You and Thea? Lord, wait until I tell Cilla."

The murderous look Colt aimed at him only made Boyd's grin widen.

"I can't thank you enough for your support here, Fletch."

Boyd gamely swallowed another chuckle, but he couldn't defeat the grin. "Oh, you've got it, pal. All the way. It's just that I never thought I'd be using the word *marriage* in the same sentence with *Colt Nightshade.* Or *Althea Grayson,* for that matter. Believe me, I'm with you all the way."

Inside the interrogation room, Althea continued to wear down her quarry. She scented his fear, and used it ruthlessly.

"You know, Leo, a little cooperation would go a long way."

"Sure, a long way to seeing me greased like Wild Bill."

Althea inclined her head. "As much as it pains me to offer it, you'd have protection."

"Right." Leo snorted out smoke. "You think I want cops on my butt twenty-four hours a day? You think it would work if I did?"

"Maybe not." She used her disinterest as another tool, slowing down the pace of the interview until Leo was squirming in his chair. "But, then again, no cooperation, no shield. You go out of here naked, Leo."

"I'll take my chances."

"That's fine. You'll make bail on the drug charges—probably deal them down so you won't do any time to speak of. But it's funny how word spreads on the street, don't you think?" She let that thought simmer in his brain. "Interested parties already know you've been tagged, Leo. And when you walk out, they won't be real sure about what you might have spilled while you were inside."

"I didn't tell you anything. I don't know anything."

"That's too bad. Because it might work against you, this ignorance. You see, we're closing in, and those same interested parties might wonder if you helped out." Casually she opened a file and revealed the police sketches. "They might wonder if I got the descriptions of these suspects from you."

"I didn't give you anything." Sweat popped out

on Leo's forehead as he stared at the sketches. "I never seen those guys before."

"Well, that may be. But I'd have to say—if the subject came up—that I talked with you. A long time. And that I have detailed sketches of suspects. You know, Leo," she added, leaning toward him, "some people add two and two and get five. Happens all the time."

"That ain't legal." He moistened his lips. "It's blackmail."

"Don't hurt my feelings. You want me to be your friend, Leo." She nudged the sketches toward him. "You see, it's all a matter of attitude, and whether or not I care if you walk out of here and end up a smear on the sidewalk. Can't say I do at the moment." She smiled, chilling him. "Now, if you were my friend, I'd do everything I could to make sure you lived a long and happy life. Maybe not in Denver, maybe someplace new. You know, Leo, a change of scene can work wonders. Change your name, change your life."

Something flickered in his eyes. She knew it was doubt. "You talking witness protection program?"

"I could be. But if I'm going to ask for something that big, I have to be able to prime the pump."

When he hesitated, she sighed. "You'd better choose sides, pal. Remember Wild Bill? All he did was meet a guy. They might have been talking about the Broncos' chances for the Superbowl. Nobody gave him the benefit of the doubt. They just iced him."

The fear was back, running in the sweat down his temples. "I get immunity. And you drop the drug charges."

"Leo, Leo…" Althea shook her head. "A smart man like you knows how life works. You give me something, if it's good enough, I give you something back. It's the American way."

He licked his lips again, lit yet another cigarette. "Maybe I've seen these two before."

"These two?" Althea tapped the sketches, and then, like Colt's cat, she pounced. "Tell me."

It was 2:00 a.m. before she was finished. She'd questioned Leo, listened to his long, rambling story, made notes, made him backtrack, repeat, expand. Then she'd called in a police stenographer and had Leo go over the same ground again, making an official statement for the tape.

She was energized as she strode back to her office. She had names now, names to run through the computer. She had threads—thin threads, perhaps, but threads nonetheless, tying an organization together.

Much of what Leo had told her was speculation and gossip. But Althea knew that a viable investigation could be built on less.

Peeling off her jacket, she sat at her desk and booted up her computer. She was peering at the screen when Colt walked in and stuck a cup under her nose.

"Thanks." She sipped, winced and spared him a glance. "What is this? It tastes like a meadow."

"Herbal tea," he told her. "You've had enough coffee."

"Nightshade, you're not going to spoil our relationship by thinking you have to take care of me, are you?" She set the cup aside and went back to the screen.

"You're wired, Lieutenant."

"I know how much I can take before the system overloads. Aren't you the one who keeps saying time's what we don't have?"

"Yeah." From his position behind her chair, he lowered his hands to her shoulders and began to rub. "You did a hell of a job with Leo," he said before she could shrug his hands off. "If I ever decide to go back to law, I'd hate to have you take on one of my clients."

"More compliments." His fingers were magic, easing without weakening, soothing without softening. "I didn't get as much as I wanted, but I think I got all he had."

"He's small-time," Colt agreed. "Passing a little business to the big boys, taking his commission."

"He doesn't know the main player. I'm sure he was telling the truth about that. But he ID'd the two Meena described. Remember the cameraman she'd told us about—the big African-American? Look." She gestured toward the screen. "Matthew Dean Scott, alias Dean Miller, alias Tidal Wave Dean."

"Catchy."

"He played some semipro football about ten years ago. Made a career out of unnecessary roughness. He broke an opposing quarterback's leg."

"These things happen."

"After the game."

"Ah, a poor sport. What else have we got on him?"

"I'll tell you what else *I've* got on him," she said, but she couldn't resist leaning back against his

massaging hands. "He was fired for breaking train-
ing—having a woman in his room."

"Boys will be boys."

"This particular woman was tied up and screaming her lungs out. They dealt it down from rape to
assault, but Scott's football days were over. After
that, we've got him on a couple more assaults, in-
decent exposure, drunk and disorderly, petty lar-
ceny, lewd behavior." She punched another button
on the key-board. "That was up to four years ago.
After that, nothing."

"You figure he turned over a new leaf? Became
a pillar of the community?"

"Sure, just like I believe men read girlie magazines because of the erudite articles."

"That's what motivates me." Grinning, he
leaned down to kiss the top of her head.

"I bet. We've got a similar history on contest-
ant number two," she continued. "Harry Kline, a
small-time actor from New York whose rap sheet
includes drunk and disorderly, possession, sexual
assault, several DWIs. He drifted into porno films
about eight years ago, and was, incredibly enough,
fired from several jobs because of his violent and
erratic behavior. He headed west, got a few similar gigs in California, then was arrested for raping

one of his costars. The defense pleaded it down and, due to the victim's line of work, made it all go away. The victim's only justice came from the fact that Harry was finished in film—blue or otherwise. Nobody even partially legit would touch him. That was five years ago. There's been nothing on him since."

"Once again, one would think our friends either became solid citizens or died in their sleep."

"Or found a handy hole to hide in. Leo claimed that he was first approached—by Kline—two, maybe three years ago. He knows it was at least two. Kline wanted women, young women who were interested in making private films. Citing free enterprise, Leo obliged him and took his commission. The number he was given to contact Kline is out of service. I'll run it through the phone company to see if it was the penthouse or another location."

"He never saw the other man, the one Meena said sat off in the corner?"

"No. His only contacts were Scott and Kline. Apparently Scott would drop in for a few drinks and brag about how good he was with a camera, and how much money he was pulling in."

"And about the girls," Colt said under his breath.

The fingers rubbing Althea's shoulders went rigid. "How he and his friends had— How did he put it? The pick of the litter?"

"Don't think about it." Instinctively she lifted a hand to cover his. "Don't, Colt. You'll mess up if you do. We're a big step closer to finding her. That's what you have to concentrate on."

"I am." He turned away and paced to the far wall. "I'm also concentrating on the fact that if I find out either of those slime touched Liz, I'm going to kill them." He turned back, his eyes blank. "You won't stop me, Thea."

"Yes, I will." She rose and went to him to take both of his fisted hands in hers. "Because I understand how much you'll want to. And that if you do, it won't change what happened. It won't help Liz. But we'll cross that bridge after we find her." She gave his hands a hard squeeze. "Don't go renegade on me now, Nightshade. I'm just starting to like working with you."

He pulled himself back, let himself look down at her. Though her eyes were shadowed and her cheeks were pale with fatigue, he could feel energy vibrating from her. She was offering him something. Compassion—with restrictions, of course. And hope, without any. The viciousness of his anger faded into the very human need for the comfort of contact.

"Althea…" His hands relaxed. "Let me hold you, will you?" She hesitated, her brow lifting in surprise. He could only smile. "You know, I'm beginning to read you pretty well. You're worried about your professional image, snuggling up against a guy in your office." Sighing, he brushed a hand through her hair. "Lieutenant, it's almost three in the morning. There's nobody here to see. And I really need to hold you."

Once again she let instinct rule, and she moved into his arms. Every time, she mused as she settled her head in the curve of his neck, every time they stood like this, they fitted perfectly. And each time it was easier to admit it.

"Feel better?" she asked, and felt him move his head against her hair.

"Yeah. He didn't know anything about Lacy, the girl who's missing?"

"No." Without thinking, she stroked his back, soothing muscles there as he had soothed hers. "And when I mentioned the possibility of murder, he was genuinely shaken. He wasn't faking that. That's why I'm certain he gave us everything he had."

"The house in the mountains." Colt let his eyes close. "He couldn't give us much."

"West or maybe north of Boulder, near a lake." She moved her shoulders. "It's a little better than we had before. We'll narrow it down, Colt."

"I feel like I'm not putting the pieces together."

"We're putting the pieces we have together," she told him. "And you're feeling that way because you're tired. Go home." She eased back so that she could look up at him. "Get some sleep. We'll start fresh in the morning."

"I'd rather go home with you."

Amused, exasperated, she could only shake her head. "Don't you ever quit?"

"I didn't say I expected to, only that I'd rather." Lifting his hands, he framed her face, stroking his thumbs over her cheekbones, then back to her temples. "I want time with you, Althea. Time when there isn't so much on my mind, or on yours. Time to be with you, and time to figure out what it is about you, just you, that makes me start thinking of long-term, permanent basis."

Instantly wary, she backed out of his arms. "Don't start that now, Nightshade."

Instantly relaxed, he grinned. "That sure does make you nervous. I never knew anyone so spooked by the thought of marriage—unless it was me. Makes me wonder why—and whether I should just sweep you right off your feet and find out the reasons after I've got a ring on your finger. Or—" he moved toward her, backing her against the desk "—if I should take things real slow, real easy, sliding you into the *I do*'s so slick that you wouldn't know you were hitched until it was over and done."

"Either way, you're being ridiculous." There was something lodged in her throat. Althea recognized it as nerves, and bitterly resented it. Feigning indifference, she picked up the tea and sipped. Now it tasted like cold flowers. "It's late," she said. "You go ahead. I can requisition a unit and drive myself home."

"I'll take you." He caught her chin in his hand and waited until her eyes were level with his. "And I mean that, Thea. Any way I can get you. But you're right—it's late. And I owe you."

"You don't—" Her denial ended on a moan when his mouth swooped down to cover hers.

She tasted frustration in the kiss, a jagged need that was barely restrained. And most difficult of all to resist, she tasted the sweetness of affection, like a thin, soothing balm over the pulsing heat.

"Colt." Even as she murmured his name against his mouth, she knew she was losing. Her arms had already lifted to wrap around him, to bring him closer, to accept and to demand.

Her body betrayed her. Or was it her heart? She could no longer tell the two apart, as the needs of one so closely matched the needs of the other. Her fingers dug deep into his shoulders as she struggled to regain her balance. Then they went lax as she allowed herself one moment of madness.

It was Colt who drew back—for himself, and for her. She'd become more important than the satisfactions of the moment. "I owe you," he said again, carefully spacing the words as he stared down into her eyes. "If I didn't, I wouldn't let you go tonight. I don't think I could. I'll drive you home." He picked up her jacket, offered it to her. "Then I'm probably going to spend the rest of the night wondering what it would have been like if I'd just locked that door there and let nature take its course."

Shaken, she draped her jacket over her shoulders before walking to the door. But she'd be damned if she'd be outdone or outmaneuvered. She paused and sent one slow smile over her shoulder. "I'll tell you what it would have been like, Nightshade. It would have been like nothing you've ever experienced. And when I'm ready—if I'm ever ready—I'll prove it."

Stunned by the punch of that single cool smile, he watched her saunter off. Letting out a long breath, he pressed a hand to the knot in his gut. Sweet God, he thought, this was the woman for him. The only woman for him. And damned if *he* wasn't ready to prove it.

With four hours' sleep, two cups of black coffee and a cherry Danish under her belt, Althea was ready to roll. By 9:00 a.m., she was at her desk, putting through a call to the telephone company with an official request for a check on the number she'd gotten from Leo. By 9:15, she had a name and address, and the information that the customer had cancelled the service only forty-eight hours before.

Though she didn't expect to find anything, she was putting in a request for a search warrant when Colt walked in.

"You don't let moss grow under your feet, do you?"

Althea hung up the phone. "I don't let anything grow under my feet. I've got a line on the number from Leo. The customer canceled the service. I imagine we'll find the place cleaned out, but I can pick up a search warrant within the hour."

"That's what I love about you, Lieutenant—no wasted moves." He eased a hip down on her desk—and was delighted to discover she smelled as good as she looked. "How'd you sleep?"

She slanted a look up at him. Direct challenge. "Like a rock. You?"

"Never better. I woke up this morning with a whole new perspective. Can you be ready to roll by noon?"

"Roll where?"

"This idea I had. I ran it by Boyd, and he—" He scowled down at her shrilling phone. "How many times a day does that ring?"

"Often enough." She plucked up the receiver. "Grayson. Yes, this is Lieutenant Althea Grayson." Her head snapped up. "Jade." With a nod for Colt, Althea covered the receiver. "Line two," she whispered. "And keep your mouth shut." She continued to listen as Colt shot from the room to pick up an extension. "Yes, we have been looking for you. I appreciate you calling in. Can you tell me where you are?"

"I'd rather not." Jade's voice was thin, jumping with nerves. "I only called because I don't want any trouble. I'm getting a job and everything. A straight job. If there's trouble with the cops, I'll lose it."

"You're not in any trouble. I contacted your mother because you can be of some help on a case I'm investigating." Althea swiveled her chair to the right so that she could see Colt through the doorway. "Jade, you remember Liz, don't you? The girl whose parents you wrote?"

"I…I guess. Maybe."

"It took a lot of courage to write that letter, and to get out of the situation you'd found yourself in. Liz's parents are very grateful to you."

"She was a nice kid. Didn't really know the score, you know? She wanted out." Jade paused, and Althea heard the sound of a scraping match, a deep intake of breath. "Listen, there was nothing I could do for her. We only had a couple of minutes alone once or twice. She slipped me the address, asked me if I'd write her folks. Like I said, she was a nice kid in a bad spot."

"Then help me find her. Tell me where they've got her."

"I don't know. Man, I really don't. They took a couple of us up in the mountains a few times. Really out there, you know. Wilderness stuff. They had this really classy cabin, though. First-rate, with a Jacuzzi, and a big stone fireplace, and this big-screen TV."

"Which way did you go out of Denver? Can you remember that?"

"Well, yeah, sort of. It was like Route 36, toward Boulder, but we just kept going on it forever. Then we took this other little road for a while. Not a highway. One of those two-lane winding jobs."

"Do you remember going by any towns? Anything that sticks out in your mind?"

"Boulder. After that there wasn't much."

"Did you go up in the morning, afternoon, night?"

"The first time it was in the morning. We got a really early start."

"After Boulder, was the sun in front of you, or behind?"

"Oh, I get it. Ah…I guess it was kind of behind us."

Althea continued to press for details, about the location, the routine, descriptions of the people Jade had seen. As a witness, Jade proved vague but cooperative. Still, Althea had no problem recognizing Scott and Kline from Jade's descriptions. There was again a mention of a man who stayed in the background, keeping to the shadows, watching.

"He was creepy, you know?" Jade continued. "Like a spider, just hanging there. The job paid good, so I went back a couple of times. Three hundred for one day, and a fifty-dollar bonus if they needed you for two. I… You know you just can't make that kind of money on the street."

"I know. But you stopped going."

"Yeah, because sometimes they got really rough. I had bruises all over me, and one of the guys even split my lip while we were doing this scene. I got scared, because it didn't seem like they were acting. It seemed like they wanted to hurt you. I told Wild Bill, and he said how I shouldn't go back. And that he wasn't going to send any more girls. He said he was going to do some checking into it, and if it was bad, he was going to talk to his cop. I knew that was you, so that's why I called back when I got the message. Bill thinks you're okay."

Wearily Althea rubbed a hand over her brow. She didn't tell Jade that she should be using the past tense as far as Wild Bill was concerned. She didn't have the heart. "Jade, you said something in your letter about thinking they'd killed one of the girls."

"I guess I did." Her voice quavered, weakened. "Listen, I'm not going to testify or anything. I'm not going back there."

"I can't promise anything, only that I'll try to keep you out of it. Tell me why you think they killed one of the girls."

"I told you how they could get rough. And it wasn't no playacting, either. The last time I was up, they really hurt me. That's when I decided I wasn't going back. But Lacy, that's a girl I hung with some, she said how she could handle it, and how the money was too good to pass up. She went up again, but she never came back. I never saw her again."

She paused, another match scraped. "It's not like I can prove anything. It's just… She left all her stuff in her room, 'cause I checked. Lacy was real fond of her things. She had this collection of glass animals. Real pretty, crystal, like. She wouldn't have left them behind. She'd have come back for them, if she could. So I thought she was dead, or they were keeping her up there, like with Liz. And I figured I better split before they tried something with me."

"Can you give me Lacy's full name, Jade? Any other information about her?"

"She was just Lacy. That's all I knew. But she was okay."

"All right. You've been a lot of help. Why don't you give me a number where I can contact you?"

"I don't want to. Look, I've told you all I know. I want out of it. I told you, I'm starting over out here."

Althea didn't press. It was a simple matter to get the number from the phone company. "If you think of anything else, no matter how insignificant it seems, will you call me back?"

"I guess. Look, I really hope you get the kid out of there, and give those creeps what they deserve."

"We will. Thanks."

"Okay. Say hi to Wild Bill."

Before Althea could think of a reply, Jade broke the connection. When she looked up, Colt was standing in her doorway. His eyes held that blank, dangerous look again.

"You can get her back here. Material witness."

"Yeah, I could." Althea dialed the phone again. She'd get the number now. Keep it for backup. "But I won't." She held up a hand for silence before Colt could speak, and made the official request to the operator.

"A 212 area code," Colt noted as Althea scribbled on her pad. "You can get the NYPD to pick her up."

"No," she said simply, then slipped the pad into her purse and rose.

"Why the hell not?" Colt grabbed her arm as she reached for her coat. "If you can get that much out of her on the phone, you'd get that much more face-to-face."

"It's because I got that much out of her." Resentful of his interference, she jerked away. "She gave me everything she had, just for the asking. No threats, no promises, no maneuvering. I asked, she answered. I don't betray trusts, Nightshade. If I need her to drop the hammer on these bastards, then I'll use her. But not until then, and not if there's another way. And not," she added deliberately, "without her consent. Is that clear?"

"Yeah." He scrubbed his hands over his face. "Yeah, it's clear. And you're right. So, you want to pick up that warrant, check that other address?"

"Yes. Do you intend to tag along?"

"You bet. We should have just enough time to finish that before we take off."

She stopped in the doorway. "Take off?"

"That's right, Lieutenant. You and I are taking a little trip. I'll tell you all about it on the way."

Chapter 8

"I think we've all lost our minds." Althea gripped her seat as the nose of the Cessna rose into the soft autumn sky.

Comfortable at the controls, Colt spared her a glance. "Come on, tough stuff, don't you like planes?"

"Sure I like planes." A tricky patch of cross-currents sent the Cessna rocking. "But I like them with flight attendants."

"There's stuff in the galley. Once we level off, you can serve yourself."

That wasn't precisely what she'd meant, but Althea said nothing, just watched the land tilt away.

She enjoyed flying, really. It was just that she had a routine. She would strap in, adjust her headset to the music of her choice, open a book and zone out for the length of the flight.

She didn't like to think of all the gauges over which she had no control.

"I still think this is a waste of time."

"Boyd didn't argue," Colt pointed out. "Look, Thea, we know the general location of the cabin. I studied that damn tape until my eyes bugged out. I'll recognize it when I see it, and plenty of the surrounding landmarks. This is worth a shot."

"Maybe" was all she'd give him.

"Think about it." Colt banked the plane and set his course. "They know the heat's on. That's why they pulled out of the penthouse. They're going to be wondering where that tape ended up, and if they try to contact Leo, they won't find him, since you've got him stashed in a safe house."

"So they'll stay out of Denver," she agreed. The engines were an irritating roar in her ears. "They might even pull up stakes and move on."

"That's just what I'm afraid of." Colt's mouth thinned as they left Denver behind. "What happens to Liz if they do? None of the options have a happy ending."

"No." That, and Boyd's approval, had convinced her to go with Colt. "No, they don't."

"I have to think they'd stick to the cabin for the time being. Even if they figure we know it exists, they wouldn't think we'd know its location. They don't know about Jade."

"I'll give you that, Nightshade. But it seems to me that you're relying on blind luck to guide you there."

"I've been lucky before. Better?" he asked when the plane leveled. "It's pretty up here, don't you think?"

There was snow on the peaks to the north, and there were broad, flat valleys between the ridges. They were cruising low enough that she could make out cars along the highway, communities that were little huddles of houses, and the deep, thick green of the forest to the west.

"It has its points." A thought erupted in her mind, making her swivel her head in his direction. "Do you have a pilot's license, Nightshade?"

He glanced over, stared, then nearly collapsed with laughter. "Lord, I'm crazy about you, Lieutenant. Do you want one of those big blowout weddings or the small, intimate kind?"

"You're crazy, period," she muttered, and

shifted deliberately to stare out through the windscreen. She'd check on his license when they got back to Denver. "And you said you weren't going to bring up that kind of thing."

"I lied." He said it cheerfully. Despite the worry that never quite dissipated, he didn't think he'd ever felt better in his life. "I've got a problem with that. A woman like you could probably cure me of it."

"Try a psychiatrist."

"Thea, we're going to make a hell of a pair. Wait until my family gets a load of you."

"I'm not meeting your family." She attributed the sudden hollowness in her stomach to another spot of turbulence.

"Well, you're probably right about that—at least until we're ready to walk down the aisle. My mother tends to manage everything, but you can handle her. My father likes spit and polish, which means the two of you would get along like bacon and eggs. A regulation type, that's the admiral."

"Admiral?" she repeated, despite her vow to remain stubbornly silent.

"Navy man. Broke his heart when I joined the air force." Colt shrugged. "That's probably why I did it. Then I have this aunt… Well, better you should meet them for yourself."

"I'm not meeting your family," she said again, annoyed that the statement sounded more petulant than firm. She unstrapped herself and marched back into the tiny galley, rooting about until she found a can of nuts and a bottle of mineral water. Curiosity had her opening the small refrigerated compartment and studying a tin of caviar and a bottle of Beaujolais. "Whose plane is this?"

"Some friend of Boyd's. A weekend jockey who likes to take women up."

Her answer to that was a grunt as she came back to take her seat. "Must be Frank the lecher. He's been after me to fly the sexy skies for years." She chose a cashew.

"Oh, yeah? Not your type?"

"He's so obvious. But then, men tend to be."

"I'll have to remind myself to be subtle. You going to share those?"

She offered the can. "Is that Boulder?"

"Yep. I'm going to track northwest from here, circle around some. Boyd tells me he has a cabin up here."

"Yes. Lots of people do. They like to escape from the city on weekends and tramp through the snow."

"Not your speed?"

"I don't see any purpose for snow unless you're skiing. And the main purpose of skiing, as far as I'm concerned, is coming back to a lodge and having hot buttered rum in front of a fire."

"Ah, you're the adventurous type."

"I live for adventure. Actually, Boyd's place does have a nice view," she admitted. "And the kids get a big kick out of it."

"So you've been there."

"A few times. I like it better in late spring, early summer, when there isn't much chance of the roads being closed." She glanced down at the patchy snow in the foothills. "I hate the thought of being stuck."

"It might have its advantages."

"Not for me." She was silent for a time, watching hills and trees take over from city and suburbs. "It is pretty," she conceded. "Especially from up here. Like a segment on public television."

He grinned at that. "Nature at a distance? I thought city girls always yearned for a country retreat."

"Not this city girl. I'd rather—" There was a violent bump that sent nuts flying and had Althea grabbing for a handhold. "What the hell was that?"

Narrow-eyed, Colt studied his gauges while he

fought to bring the nose of the plane back up. "I don't know."

"You don't know? What do you mean, you don't know? You're supposed to know!"

"Shh!" He tilted his head to listen hard to the engines. "We're losing pressure," he said, with the icy calm that had kept him alive in war-torn jungles, in deserts and in skies alive with flak.

Once she understood that the trouble was serious, Althea responded in kind. "What do we do?"

"I'm going to have to set her down."

Althea looked down, studying the thick trees and rocky hills fatalistically. "Where?"

"According to the map, there's a valley a few degrees east." Colt adjusted the course, fighting the wheel as he jiggled switches. "Watch for it," he ordered, then flipped on his radio. "Boulder tower, this is Baker Able John three."

"There." Althea pointed to what looked to be a very narrow spit of flat land between jagged peaks. Colt nodded, and continued to inform the tower of his situation.

"Hang on," he told her. "It's going to be a little rough."

She braced herself, refusing to look away as the

land rushed up to meet them. "I heard you were good, Nightshade."

"You're about to find out." He cut speed, adjusting for the drag of currents as he finessed the plane toward the narrow valley.

Like threading a needle, Althea thought. Then she sucked in her breath at the first vicious thud of wheels on land. They bounced, teetered, shook, then rolled to a gentle halt.

"You okay?" Colt asked instantly.

"Yeah." She let out a breath. Her stomach was inside out, but apart from that she thought she was all in one piece. "Yeah, I'm fine. You?"

"Dandy." He reached out, grabbed her face in both of his hands and dragged her, straining against her seat belt, close enough to kiss. "By damn, Lieutenant," he said, and kissed her again, hard. "You never flinched. Let's elope."

"Can it." When a woman was used to level emotions, it was difficult to know what to do when she had the urge to laugh and scream simultaneously. She shoved him away. "You want to let me out of this thing? I could use some solid ground under my feet."

"Sure." He released the door, even helped her alight. "I'm going to radio in our position," he told her.

"Fine." Althea took a deep gulp of fresh, cold air and tried out her legs. Not too wobbly, she discovered, pleased. All in all, she'd handled her first—and hopefully last—forced landing rather well. She had to give Colt credit, she mused as she looked around. He'd chosen his spot, and he'd made it work.

She didn't get down on her knees and kiss the ground, but she was grateful to feel it under her. As an added bonus, the view was magnificent. They were cupped between mountain and forest, sheltered from the wind, low enough to look up at the snow cascading down from the rocky peaks without being inconvenienced by it.

There was a good clean scent to the air, a clear blue sky overhead, and a bracing chill that stirred the blood. With any luck, a rescue could be accomplished within the hour, so she could afford to enjoy the scenery without being overwhelmed by the solitude.

She was feeling in tune with the world when she heard Colt clamber out of the cockpit. She even smiled at him.

"So, when are they coming to get us?"

"Who?"

"Them. Rescue people. You know, those selfless

heroes who get people out of tricky situations such as this."

"Oh, them. They're not." He dropped a tool chest on the ground, then went back inside for a short set of wooden steps.

"Excuse me?" Althea managed when she found her voice. She knew it was an illusion, but the mountains suddenly seemed to loom larger. "Did you say no one's coming to get us? Isn't the radio working?"

"Works fine." Colt climbed on the steps and uncovered the engine. He'd already stuck a rag in the back pocket of his jeans. "I told them I'd see if I could do the repairs on-site and keep in contact."

"You told them—" She moved fast, before either of them understood her intention. Her first swing caught him in the kidneys and had him tumbling off the steps. "You *idiot!* What do you mean, you'll do the repairs?" She swung again, but he dodged, more baffled than annoyed. "This isn't a Ford broken down on the highway, Nightshade. We haven't got a damn flat tire."

"No," he said carefully, braced and ready for her next move. "I think it's the carburetor."

"You think it's—" Her breath whistled out through her teeth, and her eyes narrowed. "That's it. I'm going to kill you with my bare hands."

She launched herself at him. Colt made a split-second decision, pivoted, and let her momentum carry them both to the ground. It only took him another second to realize the lady was no slouch at hand-to-hand. He took one on the chin that snapped his teeth together. It looked like it was time to get serious.

He scissored his legs around her and managed, after a short, grunting tussle, to roll her onto her back. "Hold on, will you? Somebody's going to get hurt!"

"You're damn right."

Since reason wouldn't work, he used his weight, levering himself over her as he cuffed her wrists with his hands. She bucked twice, then went still. They both knew she was only biding her time until she found an opening.

"Listen." He gave himself another moment to catch his breath, then spoke directly into her ear. "It was the most logical alternative."

"That's bull."

"Let me explain. If you still disagree afterward, we'll go for two falls out of three. Okay?" When she didn't respond, Colt set his teeth. "I want your word you won't take another punch at me until I finish."

It was a pity he couldn't see her expression at that moment. "Fine," Althea said tightly. Cautious, Colt eased back until he could watch her face. He was halfway into a sitting position when she brought her knee solidly into his crotch.

He didn't have the breath to curse her as he rolled into a ball.

"That wasn't a punch," she pointed out. She took the time to smooth back her hair, brush down her parka, before she rose. "Okay, Nightshade, let's hear it."

He only lifted a hand, made a couple of woofing noises, and waited for the stars to fade from behind his eyes. "You may have endangered our bloodline, Thea." He got creakily to his knees, breathing shallowly. "You fight dirty."

"It's the only way to fight. Spill it."

As his strength returned, he shot her a killing look. "I owe you. I owe you big. We're not injured," he ground out. "At least I wasn't until you started on me. The plane's undamaged. If you'll take a look around, you'll see that there isn't room to land another plane safely. They could send a copter, lift us out, but for what? Odds are, if I make a few minor adjustments I can fly us out."

Maybe it made sense, Althea thought. Maybe.

But it didn't alter one simple fact. "You should have consulted me. I'm here, too, Nightshade. You had no right to make that decision on your own."

"My mistake." He turned to walk—limp—back to the steps. "I figured you were the logical type and, being a public servant, wouldn't want to see other public servants pulled out for an unnecessary rescue. And, damn it, Liz might be over that ridge." With a violent clatter, he pulled a wrench from the toolbox. "I'm not going back without her."

Oh, he would have to push that button, Althea thought as she turned away to stare into the deep green of the neighboring forest. He would have to let her hear that terrible worry in his voice, see the fire of it in his eyes.

He would have to be perfectly and completely right.

Pride was the hardest of all pills to swallow. Making the effort, she turned back and walked to stand beside the steps. "I'm sorry. I shouldn't have lost my temper."

His response was a grunt.

"Does it still hurt?"

He looked back down at her then, with a gleam in his eyes that would have made lesser women grovel. "Only when I breathe."

She smiled and patted his leg. "Try to think about something else. Do you want me to hand you tools or something?"

His eyes only narrowed further, until they were thin blue slits. "Do you know the difference between a ratchet and a torque wrench?"

"No." She tossed her hair back. "Why should I? I have a perfectly competent mechanic to look after my car."

"And if you break down on the highway?"

She sent him a pitying look. "What do you think?"

He ground his teeth and went back to the carburetor. "If I made a comment like that, you'd call it sexist."

She grinned behind his back, but when she spoke, her voice was sober. "Why is calling a tow truck sexist? I think there's some instant coffee in the galley," she continued. "I'll make some."

"It isn't smart to use the battery," he muttered. "We'll make do with soft drinks."

"No problem."

When she returned twenty minutes later, Colt was cursing the engine. "This friend of Boyd's should be shot for taking such haphazard care of his equipment."

"Are you going to fix it or not?"

"Yeah, I'm going to fix it." He found several interesting names to call a bolt he was fighting to loosen. "It's just going to take a little longer than I expected." Prepared for some pithy comment, he glanced down. She merely stood there patiently, the breeze ruffling her hair. "What's that?" he asked, nodding down at her hands.

"I think it's called a sandwich." She held up the bread and cheese for his inspection. "Not much of one, but I thought you might be hungry."

"Yeah, I am." The gesture mollified him somewhat. He lifted his hands and showed her palms and fingers streaked with grease. "I'm a little handicapped."

"Okay. Bend over." When he obeyed, she brought the bread to his mouth. They watched each other over it as he took a bite.

"Thanks."

"You're welcome. I found a beer." She pulled the bottle out of her pocket and tipped it back. "We'll share." Then she held it to his lips.

"Now I know I love you."

"Just eat." She fed him more of the sandwich. "Do you have any idea how much longer it's going to take you to get us airborne?"

"Yeah." And because he did, he made sure he got his full share of the beer and the sandwich before he told her. "It'll be an hour, maybe two."

She blinked. "Two hours? We'll have run out of daylight by then. You don't plan to fly this out of here in the dark?"

"No, I don't." Though he remained braced for a sneak attack, he went back to the engine. "It'll be safer to wait until morning."

"Until morning," she repeated, staring at his back. "And just what are we supposed to do until morning?"

"Pitch a tent, for starters. There's one in the cabin, in the overhead. I guess old Frank likes to take his ladies camping."

"That's great. Just great. You're telling me we have to sleep out here?"

"We could sleep in the plane," he pointed out. "But it wouldn't be as comfortable, or as warm, as stretching out in a tent beside a fire." He began to whistle as he worked. He'd said he owed her one. He hadn't realized he'd be able to pay her back so soon, or so well. "I don't suppose you know how to start a campfire."

"No, I don't know how to start a damn campfire."

"Weren't you ever a Girl Scout?"

She made a sound like steam escaping a funnel. "No. Were you?"

"Can't say I was—but I was friendly with a few of them. Well, you go on and gather up some twigs, darling. I'll talk you through your first merit badge."

"I am not going to gather twigs."

"Okay, but it's going to get cold once that sun goes down. A fire keeps the chill—and other things—away."

"I'm not—" She broke off, looked uneasily around. "What other things?"

"Oh, you know. Deer, elk…wildcats…"

"Wildcats." Her hand went automatically to her shoulder rig. "There aren't any wildcats around here."

He lifted his head and glanced around as if considering. "Well, it might be too early in the year yet. But they do start coming down from the higher elevations near winter. Of course, if you want to wait until I've finished here, I'll get a fire going. May be dark by then, though."

He was doing it on purpose. She was sure of it. But then again… She cast another look around, toward the forest, where the shadows were lengthening. "I'll get the damn wood," she muttered, and stomped off toward the trees. After she checked her weapon.

He watched her, smiling. "We're going to do just fine together," he said to himself. "Just fine."

Following Colt's instructions, Althea managed to start a respectable fire within a circle of stones. She didn't like it, but she did it. Then, because he claimed to be deeply involved in the final repairs to the plane, she was forced to rig the tent.

It was a lightweight bubble that Colt declared would nearly erect itself. After twenty minutes of struggle and swearing, she had it up. A narrow-eyed study showed her that it would shelter the two of them—as long as they slept hip to hip.

She was still staring at it, ignoring the chill of the dusk, when she heard the engine spring to life.

"Good as new," Colt shouted, then shut off the engines. "I have to clean up," he told her. He leapt out of the cabin, holding a jug of water. He used it sparingly, along with a can of degreaser from the toolbox. "Nice job," he said, nodding toward the tent.

"Thanks a bunch."

"There are blankets in the plane. We'll do well enough." Still crouched, he drew in a deep breath, tasting smoke and pine and good, crisp air. "Nothing quite like camping out in the hills."

She shoved her hands into her pockets. "I'll have to take your word for it."

He finished scrubbing his hands with a rag before he rose. "Don't tell me you've never done any camping."

"All right, I won't tell you."

"What do you do for a vacation?"

She arched a brow. "I go to a hotel," she said precisely. "Where they have room service, hot and cold running water and cable TV."

"You don't know what you're missing."

"I suppose I'm about to find out." She shivered once, sighed. "I could use a drink."

In addition to the Beaujolais, they feasted on rich, sharp cheese, caviar and thin crackers spread with a delicate pâté.

All in all, Althea decided, it could have been worse.

"Not like any camp meal I've ever had," Colt commented as he scooped more caviar onto a cracker. "I thought I'd have to go kill us a rabbit."

"Please, not while I'm eating." Althea sipped more wine and found herself oddly relaxed. The fire did indeed keep the chill away. And it was soothing to watch it flicker and hiss. Overhead, countless stars wheeled and winked, stabbing the cloudless black sky. A quarter-moon silvered the trees and lent a glow to the snow capping the peaks that circled them.

She'd stopped jerking every time an owl hooted.

"Pretty country." Colt lit an after-dinner cigar. "I never spent much time here before."

Neither had she, Althea realized, though she'd lived in Denver for a dozen years. "I like the city," she said, more to herself than Colt. She picked up a stick to stir the fire, not because it needed it, but because it was fun to watch the sparks fly.

"Why?"

"I guess because it's crowded. Because you can find anything you want. And because I feel useful there."

"And that's important to you, feeling useful."

"Yeah, it's important."

He watched the way the flames cast shadow and light over her face, highlighting her eyes, sharpening her cheekbones, softening her skin. "It was rough on you, growing up."

"It's over." When he took her hand, she neither resisted nor responded. "I don't talk about it," she said flatly. "Ever."

"All right." He could wait. "We'll talk about something else." He brought her hand to his lips, and felt a response, just a slight flexing, then relaxing, of her fingers. "I guess you never told stories around the campfire."

She smiled. "I guess not."

"I could probably think of one—just to pass the time. Lie or truth?"

She started to laugh, but then she shot to her feet, whipping out her weapon. Colt's reaction was lightning-fast. In an instant he was beside her, shoving her back, his own gun slapped from his boot into his palm.

"What?" he demanded, his eyes narrowed and searching every shadow.

"Did you hear that? There's something out there."

He cocked an ear, while she instinctively shifted to guard his back. After a moment of throbbing silence, he heard a faint rustling, then the far-off cry of a coyote. The plaintive call had Althea's blood drumming.

Colt swore, but at least he didn't laugh. "Animals," he told her, bending to replace his gun.

"What kind?" Her eyes were still scanning the perimeter, wary, watchful.

"Small ones," he assured her. "Badgers, rabbits." He laid a hand over the ones that gripped her weapon. "Nothing you have to put a hole in, Deadeye."

She wasn't convinced. The coyote called again, and an owl hooted in counterpoint. "What about those wildcats?"

He started to respond, thought better of it, and tucked his tongue in his cheek. "Well, now, darling, they aren't likely to come too close to the fire."

Frowning, she replaced her weapon. "Maybe we should have a bigger fire."

"It's big enough." He turned her toward him, running his hands up and down her arms. "I don't think I've ever seen you so spooked."

"I don't like being this exposed. There's too much here, out here." And the sterling truth was that she would rather face a hopped-up junkie in a dark alley than one small, furry creature with fangs. "Don't grin at me, damn it!"

"Was I grinning?" He ran his tongue around his teeth and struggled to look sober. "It looks like you're going to have to trust me to get you through this."

"Oh, am I?"

He tightened his grip when she started to back

away. The look in his eyes changed so quickly, from amusement to desire, that it took her breath away. "There's just you and me, Althea."

She let the clogged air slowly out of her lungs. "It looks like."

"I don't figure I have to tell you again how I feel about you. Or how much I want you."

"No." Tension flooded into her when he brushed his lips over her temple. And heat, a frightening spear of it, stabbed up her spine.

"I can make you forget where you are." He trailed his lips down to her jawline and nibbled up the other side. "If you'll let me."

"You'd have to be damn good for that."

He laughed, because there had been a challenge in the statement, even though her breath had caught on the words. "It's a long time until morning. I'm betting I can convince you before sunrise."

Why was she resisting something she wanted so terribly? Hadn't she told herself long ago never again to let fear cloud her desires? And hadn't she learned to sate those desires without penalty?

She could do so now, with him, and erase this grinding ache.

"All right, Nightshade." Fearlessly she linked

her arms around his neck, met his eyes straight on. "I'll take that bet."

His hand fisted in her hair, dragged her head back. For one long, humming moment, they stared at each other. Then he plundered.

Her mouth was hot and honeyed under his, as demanding as hunger, as wild as the night. He plunged into the kiss, using tongue and teeth, knowing he could gorge himself on her and never be filled. So he took more, relentlessly savaging her mouth while she met demand with demand and power with power.

It was like the first time, she realized giddily. The first time he'd dragged her to him and made her taste what he had to offer. Like some fatal drug, the taste had her pulses pounding, her blood swimming fast and her mind spinning away from reason.

She wondered how she had expected to come away whole. And then she forgot to care.

She no longer wanted to be safe, to be in control. Now, here, with him, she wanted only to feel, to experience everything that had once seemed impossible, or at least unwise. And if she sacrificed survival, so be it.

Driven by greed, she tore at his coat, desperate

to feel the hard, solid body beneath. He didn't have to be stronger than she, but if he was, she would accept the vulnerability that came with being a woman. And the power that raced alongside it.

She was like a volcano ready to erupt, and she wanted nothing more than to be joined with him when the tremors came.

She was stripping him of his sanity, layer by layer. Those wild lips, those frantic hands. On an oath that was almost a prayer, he half carried, half dragged her toward the tent, feeling like some primeval hunter flinging his chosen mate into his cave.

They tumbled into the small shelter together, a tangle of limbs, a tangle of needs. He yanked her coat down her shoulders, fighting for breath as he raced greedy kisses down her throat.

He felt the vibration of her groan against his lips as he fought her shoulder rig, tearing aside that symbol of control and violence, knowing he was losing control, overwhelmed by a violence of feelings that he couldn't suppress.

He wanted her naked and straining. And screaming.

Her breath caught in gasps as she tugged, pulled, ripped, at his clothes. The firelight glowed orange through the thin material of the tent, and she could see his eyes, the dark, dangerous purpose in them. She reveled in it, in the panicked excitement that racked her body where he groped and possessed. He would ravage her tonight, she knew. And be ravaged in turn.

Levering himself back, he dragged her sweater up and over her head and tossed it aside. She wore lace beneath, a snow-white fancy that in a saner place, in a saner time, would have aroused him by its blatant femininity. He might have toyed with the straps, skimmed his fingers over her subtle peaks. Now he only ripped it apart in one jerky move to free her breasts for his greedy mouth.

The flavor of that warm, scented flesh hit his system like a blow. And her response, the lovely arching of her body against his, the long, throaty moan, the quick, helpless quiver, drove him toward a summit of pleasure he had never dreamed of.

He feasted.

A whimper caught in her throat. She dug her nails into the naked flesh of his shoulders, needing to drive him on, terrified of where he was taking her. She clutched at him for balance, moved under him in sinuous invitation, arching once more as he peeled her slacks away, skimming those impossibly clever fingers down her thighs.

The triangle of lace that shielded her tore jaggedly. Once again his mouth feasted.

Her cry of stunned release rippled through his blood. She shot up like a rocket, exploding, imploding, feeling herself scatter and burn. But where the release should have peaked and leveled, he gave her no respite. She clutched at the blanket while he battered her system with sensations that had no name, no form.

When he rose over her, every muscle trembling, he found her eyes open and on his. He watched her face, filled himself with it even as he buried himself inside her in one desperate stroke. Her eyes glazed, closed. His own vision grayed before he buried his face in her hair.

His body took over, matching the fast, furious rhythm of her hips. They rode each other like fury, greedy children gorging themselves on forbidden fruit. Her final cry of dark pleasure echoed through the air seconds before his own.

Strength sapped, he collapsed onto her, gulping in air as he felt her tremble beneath him from the aftershocks.

"Who won?" he managed after a moment.

She hadn't thought it possible to laugh at such a time, but a chuckle rumbled into her throat. "Let's call it a draw."

"Good enough for me." He thought about lifting himself off her, but was afraid he might shatter if he tried to move. "Plenty good enough. I'm going to kiss you in a minute," he murmured, "but first I have to drum up the strength."

"I can wait." Althea let her eyes close again, and savored the closeness. His body continued to radiate heat, and his heart was far from steady. She stroked her hand down his back for the simple pleasure of the contact, frowning a bit when her fingers ran over a raised scar. "What's this?"

"Hmm?" He stirred himself, surprised that he'd nearly fallen asleep on top of her. "Iraq."

She hadn't realized he'd been there. It occurred to her that there was quite a bit about him that lay in shadows. "I thought you'd retired before that started."

"I had. I agreed to do a little job—sort of a side job."

"A favor."

"You could call it that. Caught a little flak—nothing to worry about." He tilted his head, nuzzling. "You have the most gorgeous shoulders. Have I mentioned that?"

"No. Do you still do favors for the government?"

"Only if they ask nicely." He grunted and

rolled so that he could shift her on top of him. "Better?"

"Mmm…." She rested her cheek on his chest. "But I think we might freeze to death."

"Not if we keep active." He grinned when she lifted her head to look down at him. "Survival methods, Lieutenant."

"Of course." Her lips curved into a smile. "I have to say, Nightshade, I like your methods."

"That so?" Gently he combed his fingers through her hair, tested its weight with his hand.

"That's very so. How soon do we have to add wood to that fire?"

"Oh, we've got a little while yet."

"Then we shouldn't waste time, should we?" Still smiling, she lowered her mouth to his.

"Nope." He felt himself hardening again inside her, and prepared to let her take the lead. As his lips curved against hers, he was struck by a stab of love so sharp it stole his breath. He clutched her close, held on. "I know it's a tired line, Thea, but it's never been like this for me before. Not with anyone."

That frightened her, and what frightened her more than the words was the flush of warmth they brought to her. "You talk too much."

"Thea…"

But she shook her head and rose up, taking him deep inside her, tantalizing his body so that the need for words slipped away.

Chapter 9

Colt awakened quickly. An old habit. He registered his surroundings—the pale light of dawn creeping into the tent, the rough blanket and hard ground beneath his back, and the soft, slender woman curled on top of him. It made him smile, remembering the way she'd rolled over him during the night, seeking a place more comfortable than the unyielding floor of the valley.

At the time, they'd both been too exhausted to do more than cuddle up and sleep. Now the sun had brought a reminder of the outside world, and their duties in it. Still, he took a moment to enjoy the lazy intimacy, and to imagine other times, other places, where it would once again be only the two of them.

Gently he tugged the blanket over her bare shoulder and let his fingers trail down over her hair where it lay pooled across her cheek and throat.

She shifted, her eyes opening and locking on his.

"Good reflexes, Lieutenant."

She ran her tongue over her teeth, letting her mind and body adjust to the situation. "I guess it's morning."

"Right the first time. Sleep okay?"

"I've slept better." Every muscle in her body ached, but she figured a couple of aspirin and some exercise would handle that. "You?"

"Like a baby," he said. "Some of us are used to roughing it."

She only lifted a brow, then rolled off him. "Some of us want coffee." The moment she left his warmth, the chill stung her skin. Shivering, she groped for her sweater.

"Hey." Before she could bundle up in the sweater, he grabbed her around the waist and hauled her to him. "You forgot something." His hand slid up her back to cup her head as his mouth met hers.

Her body went fluid, sweetly so, and her lips parted in invitation. She could feel herself melting into him, and wondered at it. All through the night they had come together, again and again, each time like lightning, with flashes of greed. But this was softer, steadier, stronger, like a candle that remained alight long after a raging fire had burned itself out.

"You sure are nice to wake up to, Althea."

She wanted to burrow into him, to grab hold and hang on as though her life depended on it. Instead, she flicked a finger down the stubble on his chin. "You're not so bad, Nightshade."

She moved away quickly, a little too quickly, to give herself the time and space to settle. Because he was beginning to read her very well, he smiled.

"You know, once we're married, we should get ourselves one of those king-size beds, so we'll have plenty of room to roll around and get tangled up."

She tugged the sweater on. When her head emerged, her eyes were cool. "Who's making the coffee?"

He nodded thoughtfully. "That is something

we'll have to decide. Keeping those little routines straight helps a marriage run smooth."

She bit back a laugh and reached for her slacks. "You owe me some underwear."

He watched her pull the slacks up her long, smooth legs. "Buying it for you is going to be pure pleasure." He shrugged into his shirt while Althea hunted for her socks. Knowing the value of timing, he waited until she'd found them both. "Darling, I've been thinking...."

She answered with a grunt as she tugged on her shoes.

"How do you feel about getting hitched on New Year's Eve? Kind of romantic, starting out the next year as husband and wife."

This time she hissed out her breath. "I'll make the damn coffee," she muttered, and crawled out of the tent.

Colt gave her retreating bottom a friendly pat and chuckled to himself. She was coming around, he decided. She just didn't know it yet.

By the time Althea got the fire started again, she'd had more than enough of the great outdoors. Maybe it was beautiful, she thought as she rummaged through the small supply of pots they'd found on the plane. Maybe it was even magnificent, with its rugged, snow-capped peaks and densely forested slopes. But it was also cold, and hard and deserted.

They had a handful of nuts between them, and not a restaurant in sight.

Too impatient to wait until it boiled, she heated water until it was hot to the touch, then dumped in a generous amount of instant coffee. The scent was enough to make her drool.

"Now that's a pretty sight." Colt stood just outside the tent, watching her. "A beautiful woman bending over a campfire. And you do have a nice way of bending, Thea."

"Stuff it, Nightshade."

He strolled to her grinning. "Cranky before your coffee, darling?"

She knocked aside the hand he'd lifted to toy with her hair. He was charming her again, and it was just going to have to stop. "Here's breakfast." She shoved the can of nuts at him. "You can pour your own coffee."

Obligingly he crouched down and poured the mixture into two tin mugs. "Nice day," he said conversationally. "Low wind, good visibility."

"Yeah, great." She accepted the mug he offered. "God, I'd kill for a toothbrush."

"Can't help you there." He sampled the coffee, grimaced. It was mud, he decided, but at least it packed a punch. "Don't you worry, we'll be back in civilization before much longer. You can brush your teeth, have yourself a nice hot bubble bath, go to the hairdresser."

She started to smile—it was the bubble bath that did it—but then she whipped her head up and scowled. "Leave my hair out of this." Setting the mug down, she knelt and began to rummage through her purse. Once she found her brush, she sat cross-legged on the ground, her back to Colt, and began to drag it through her tangled hair.

"Here now." He sat behind her, snuggling her back into the vee of his legs. "Let me do that."

"I can do it myself."

"Yeah, but you're about to brush yourself bald." After a short tussle, he snatched the brush away. "You should take more care with this," he murmured, gently working out the tangles. "It's the most beautiful head of hair I've ever seen. Up close like this, I can see a hundred different shades of red and gold and russet."

"It's just hair." But if Althea had a point of van-

ity, Colt was stroking it now. And it felt wonderful. She couldn't resist a sigh as he brushed and
lifted, caressed and smoothed. They might be in
the middle of nowhere, but for that moment Althea
felt as though she were in the lap of luxury.

"Look," Colt whispered against her ear. "At
three o'clock."

Responding instinctively to the direction, Althea
turned her head. There, just at the verge of the forest, stood a deer. No, not a deer, she realized.
Surely no deer could be so huge. His shoulders
were nearly as high as a man, and massive. His
head was lifted, scenting the air, with his high
crown of antlers spearing upward.

"It's, ah…"

"Wapiti," Colt murmured, wrapping his arms
companionably around her waist. "American elk.
That's one beautiful bull."

"Big. Big is what he is."

"Close to seven hundred pounds, by the look of
him. There, he's caught our scent."

Althea felt her heart jolt when the elk turned his
great head and looked at her. He seemed both ar-
rogant and wise as he studied the humans who
were trespassing on his territory.

And suddenly there was an aching in her throat,

a response to beauty, a trembling deep inside, a kind of wonder. For a moment the three of them remained poised, measuring each other. A lark called, a searingly beautiful cascade of notes.

The elk turned, vanished into the shadowed trees.

"I guess he didn't want coffee and cashews," Althea said quietly. She couldn't say why she was moved. She only knew that she was, deeply. Relaxed against Colt, cradled in his arms, she was completely and inexplicably content.

"Can't say I blame him." Colt rubbed his cheek against her hair. "It's a hell of a way to start the day."

"Yeah." She turned, impulsively winding an arm around his neck, pressing her lips to his. "This is better."

"Much better," he agreed, sinking in when she deepened the kiss. He nuzzled, and was amused when she laughed and shoved his unshaven face away from the tender curve of her throat. "Once we're back in Denver, I want you to remind me where we left off."

"I might do that." With some regret, she drew away. "We'd better—what do you call it? Break camp? And, by the way," she added, shrugging into her shoulder rig, "you owe me more than new lingerie—you owe me breakfast."

"Put it on my tab."

Twenty minutes later, they were strapped into the cockpit. Colt checked his gauges while Althea applied blusher to her cheekbones.

"We ain't going to a party," he commented.

"I may not be able to brush my teeth," she said, and crunched down on a mint she'd found in her purse. "I may not be able to take a shower. But, by damn, I haven't lost all sense of propriety."

"I like your cheeks pale." He started the engines. "Kind of fragile."

After one narrow-eyed stare, she deliberately added more blusher. "Just fly, Nightshade."

"Yes, sir, Lieutenant."

He didn't see the point in telling her it would be a tricky takeoff. While she was occupied braiding her hair, he maneuvered the plane into the best position for taxiing. After touching a finger to the medal that rested under his shirt, he let her rip.

They jolted, bounced, shuddered and finally lifted, degree by degree. Colt fought the crosscurrents, dipping one wing, leveling off, nosing upward. Finally they cleared the ridge and shot over the tops of the trees.

"Not too shabby, Nightshade." Althea flipped her braid behind her back. When he glanced over, he saw the awareness in her eyes. The hands that were currently uncapping a tube of mascara were rock-steady, but she knew. He should have realized she would know.

"Boyd was right, Thea. You're a hell of a partner."

"Just try to hold this thing steady for a few minutes, will you?" Smiling to herself, she angled her purse mirror and began to do her lashes. "So, what's the plan?"

"Same as before. We circle this area. Look for cabins. The one we want has a sloped drive."

"That certainly narrows things down."

"Shut up. It's also a two-story with a covered wraparound deck and a trio of windows on the front, facing west. The sun was going down in one scene in the video," he explained. "According to the other information we have, there's a lake somewhere in the general area. I also saw fir and spruce, which gives us the elevation. The cabin was whitewashed logs. It shouldn't be that hard to spot."

He might be right about that, but Althea knew

there was something else that needed to be said. "She might not be there, Colt."

"We're going to find out." He banked the plane and headed west.

Because she could see the worry come into his eyes, Althea changed tack. "Tell me, what rank were you in the air force?"

"Major." He drummed up a smile. "Looks like I outrank you."

"You're retired," she reminded him. "I bet you looked swell in uniform."

"I wouldn't mind seeing you in dress blues. Look."

Following his direction, she spotted a cabin below. It was a three-level structure fashioned from redwood. She noted two others, separated from each other by lines of trees.

"None of them fit."

"No," he agreed. "But we'll find the one that does."

They continued to search, with Althea peering through binoculars. Hideaways were snuggled here and there, most of them seemingly unoccupied. A few had smoke puffing out of a chimney and trucks or four-wheel-drive vehicles parked outside.

Once she saw a man in a bright red shirt splitting wood. She spotted a herd of elk grazing in a frosty meadow, and the flash of white-tail deer.

"There's nothing," she said at length. "Unless we want to do a documentary on— Wait." A glint of white caught her attention, then was lost. "Circle around. Four o'clock." She continued to scan, searching the snow-dusted ridges.

And there it was, two stories of whitewashed logs, a trio of windows facing west, the deck. At the end of the sloping gravel drive sat a muscular-looking truck. As further proof of habitation, smoke was spiraling out of the chimney.

"That could be it."

"I'm betting it is." Colt circled once, then veered off.

"I might take that bet." She unhooked the radio mike. "Give me the position. I'll call it in, get a surveillance team up here so we can go back and talk a judge into issuing a warrant."

Colt gave her the coordinates. "Go ahead and call it in. But I'm not waiting for a piece of paper."

"What the hell do you think you can do?"

His eyes flashed to hers, then away. "I'm setting the plane down, and I'm going in."

"No," she said, "you're not."

"You do what you have to." He angled for the

meadow where Althea had spotted the grazing elk. "There's a good chance she's in there. I'm not leaving her."

"What are you going to do?" she demanded, too incensed to noticed the perilous descent. "Break in, guns blazing? That's movie stuff, Nightshade. Not only is it illegal, but it puts the hostage in jeopardy."

"You've got a better idea?" He braced himself. They were going to slide once the wheels hit. He hoped to God they didn't roll.

"We'll get a team up here with surveillance equipment. We figure out who owns the cabin, get the paperwork pushed through."

"Then we break in? No thanks. You said you'd been skiing, right?"

"What?"

"You're about to do it in a plane. Hold on."

She jerked her head around, gaped through the windscreen as the glittering meadow hurled toward them. She had time for an oath—a vicious one—but then she lost her breath at the impact.

They hit, and went sliding. Snow spewed up the side of the plane, splattering the windows. Althea watched almost philosophically as they hurtled toward a wall of trees. Then the plane spun in two wicked circles before coming to a grinding stop.

"You maniac!" She took deep breaths, fighting back the worst of her temper. She would have let it loose, but there wasn't enough room to maneuver in the cabin. And when she murdered him she wanted to do it right.

"I landed a plane in the Aleutians once, when the radar was down. It was a lot worse than this."

"What does that prove?" she demanded.

"That I'm still a hell of a pilot?"

"Grow up!" she shouted. "This isn't fantasyland. We're closing in on suspected kidnappers, suspected murderers, and there's very possibly an innocent kid caught in the middle. We're going to do this right, Nightshade."

With one jerk, he unstrapped himself, then grabbed both her hands at the wrists. "You listen to me." She would have winced at the way his fingers dug into her flesh, but the fury in his eyes stopped her. "I know what's real, Althea. I've seen enough reality in my life—the waste of it, and the cruelty of it. I know that girl. I held her when she was a baby, and I'm not leaving her welfare up to paperwork and procedure."

"Colt—"

"Forget it." He shoved her hands aside, jerked back. "I'm not asking for your help, because I'm trying to respect your ideas of rules and regulations. But I'm going after her, Thea, and I'm going now."

"Wait." She held up a hand, then dragged it through her hair. "Let me think a minute."

"You think too damn much." But when he started to rise, she shoved a fist into his chest.

"I said wait." Then she tipped her head back, closed her eyes and thought it through.

"How far is it to the cabin?" she asked after a moment. "Half a mile?"

"More like three-quarters."

"The roads leading in were all plowed."

"Yeah." Impatience shimmered around him. "So?"

"It would have been handier if I could have been stuck in a snowdrift. But a breakdown's good enough."

"What are you talking about?"

"I'm talking about working together." She opened her eyes, pinned him with them. "You don't like the way I work, I don't like the way you work. So we're going to have to find a middle ground. I'm calling this in, arranging to have the local police back us up, and I'm going to have them get word to Boyd. See if he can get some paperwork started."

"I told you—"

"I don't care what you told me," she said calmly. "This is how it's going down. We can't go bursting in there. Number one, we might be wrong about the cabin. Number two," she said, cutting him off again, "it puts Liz in increased jeopardy if they're holding her there. And number three, without probable cause, without proper procedure, these bastards might wiggle out, and I want them put away. Now, you listen…"

He didn't like it. It didn't matter how much sense it made or how good a plan she'd devised. But during the long trek to the cabin she defused whatever arguments he voiced with calm, simple logic.

She was going in.

"What makes you think they'll let you inside just because you ask?"

She tilted her head, slanted a look up from under her lashes. "I haven't wasted any on you, Nightshade, but I have a tremendous amount of charm at my disposal." She lengthened her stride to match his. "What do you think most men will do when a helpless woman comes knocking, begging for help because she's lost, her car's broken down and—" she gave a delicate shiver and turned her voice into a purr "—and it's so awfully cold outside."

He swore and watched his breath puff away in smoke. "What if they offer to drive you back to your car and fix it?"

"Well, I'll be terribly grateful. And I'll stall them long enough to do what needs to be done."

"And if they get rough?"

"Then you and I will have to kick butt, won't we?"

He couldn't help but look forward to that. And yet… "I still think I should go in with you."

"They're not going to be sympathetic if the little woman has a big strong man with her." Sarcasm dripped in the chilly air. "With any luck, the local boys will be here before things get nasty." She paused, judging the distance. "We're close enough. One of them might be out for a morning stroll. We don't want to be spotted together."

Colt shoved his fists into his pockets, then made them relax. She was right—more, she was good. He pulled his hands out, grabbed her shoulders and hauled her close. "Watch your step, Lieutenant."

She kissed him, hard. "Same goes."

She turned, walked away with long, ground-eating strides. He wanted to tell her to stop, to tell her he loved her. Instead, he headed over the rough ground toward the rear of the cabin. This wasn't the time to throw her any emotional curves. He'd save them for later.

Blocking everything from his mind, he sprinted through the hard-crusted snow, keeping low.

Althea moved fast. She wanted to be out of breath and a little teary-eyed when she reached the cabin. Once she came into view of the windows, she switched to a stumbling run, pantomiming relief. She all but fell against the door, calling and banging.

She recognized Kline when he opened it. He wore baggy gray sweats, and his bleary eyes were squinting against the smoke from the cigarette tucked into the corner of his mouth. He smelled of tobacco and stale whiskey.

"Oh, thank God!" Althea slumped against the doorjamb. "Thank God! I was afraid I'd never find anyone. I feel like I've been walking forever."

Kline sized her up. She was one sweet-looking babe, he decided, but he wasn't big on surprises. "What do you want?"

"My car…" She pressed a fluttering hand to her heart. "It broke down—it must be a mile from here, at least. I was coming to visit some friends. I don't know, maybe I made a wrong turn." She shuddered, wrapped her parka closer around her. "Is it all right if I come in? I'm so cold."

"There ain't nobody up around here. No other cabins near here."

She closed her eyes. "I knew I must have turned wrong somewhere. Everything starts to look the same. I left Englewood before sunup—wanted to start my vacation first thing." Staring up at him, wide-eyed, she managed a weak smile. "Some vacation so far. Look, can I just use the phone, call my friends so they can come get me?"

"I guess." The broad was harmless, Kline decided. And a pleasure to look at.

"Oh, a fire…" With a moan of relief, Althea dashed toward it. "I didn't know I could be so cold." While she rubbed her hands together, she beamed over her shoulder at Kline. "I can't thank you enough for helping me out."

"No problem." He pulled the dangling cigarette from his mouth. "We don't get much traffic up here."

"I can see why." She shifted her gaze to the windows. "Still, it is lovely. And this place!" She circled, looking dazzled. "It's just fabulous. I guess if you were all cozied up by the fire with a bottle of wine, you wouldn't mind sitting out a blizzard or two."

His lips curled. "I like to cozy up with something other than a bottle."

Althea fluttered her lashes, lowered them modestly. "It certainly is romantic, Mr—?"

"Kline. You can call me Harry."

"All right, Harry. I'm Rose," she said, giving him her middle name in case he'd recognized the name of Wild Bill's cop. She offered her hand. "It's a real pleasure. I think you've saved my life."

"What the hell's going on down there?"

Althea glanced up to the loft and saw a tall, wiry man with an untended shock of blond hair. She tagged him as the second male actor in the video.

"Got us an unexpected guest, Donner," Kline called up. "Car broke down."

"Well, hell…" Donner blinked his eyes clear and took a good look. "You're out early, sweetie."

"I'm on vacation," she said, and flashed him a smile.

"Isn't that nice?" Donner started downstairs,

preening, Althea noticed, like a rooster in a hen-house. "Why don't you fix the lady a cup of coffee, Kline?"

"Tidal Wave's already in the kitchen. It's his turn."

"Fine." Donner sent what was meant to be an intimate smile toward Althea. "Tell him to pour another cup for the lady."

"Why don't you—"

"Oh, I would *love* a cup of coffee," Althea said, turning her big brown eyes on Kline. "I'm just frozen."

"Sure." He shrugged, shot Donner a look that made Althea think of one male dog warning off a competitor, then strode off.

How many more of the organization were in the cabin? she wondered. Or was it just the three of them?

"I was just telling Harry how beautiful your house is." She wandered the living room, dropping her purse onto a table. "Do you live here year-round?"

"No, we just use it now and again."

"It's so much bigger than it looks from outside."

"It does the job." He moved closer as Althea sat on the arm of a chair. "Maybe you'd like to hang out here for your vacation."

She laughed, making no objection when he brushed a finger through her hair. "Oh, but my friends are expecting me. Still, I do have two weeks…" She laughed again, low and throaty. "Tell me, what do you guys do around here for fun?"

"You'd be surprised." Donner laid a hand on her thigh.

"I don't surprise easily."

"Back off." Kline came back in with a mug of black coffee. "Here you are, Rose."

"Thanks." She sniffed deeply, curling her shoulders in for effect. "I feel warm and toasty already."

"Why don't you take off your coat?" Donner put a hand to her collar, but she shifted, smiling.

"As soon as my insides defrost a little more." She'd taken the precaution of removing her shoulder rig, but she preferred more camouflage, as her weapon was snug at the small of her back. "Are the two of you brothers?" she asked conversationally.

Kline snorted. "Not hardly. You could say we're partners."

"Oh, really? What kind of business are you in?"

"Communications," Donner stated, flashing white teeth.

"That's fascinating. You sure have a lot of

equipment." She glanced toward the big-screen TV, the state-of-the-art VCR/DVD and stereo. "I love watching movies on long winter nights. Maybe we can get together sometime and…" She let her words trail off, alerted by a movement at the back of the loft. Glancing up, she saw the girl.

Her hair was tousled, and her eyes were unbearably tired. She'd lost weight, Althea thought, but she recognized Liz from the snapshot Colt had shown her.

"Why, hello there," she said, and smiled.

"Get back in your room," Kline snapped. "Now."

Liz moistened her lips. She was wearing tattered jeans and a bright blue sweater that was tattered at the cuffs. "I wanted some breakfast." Her voice was quiet, Althea noted, but not cowed.

"You'll get it." He glanced back at Althea, satisfied that she was smiling with friendly disinterest. "Now get on back to your room until I call you."

Liz hesitated, long enough to aim one cold glare at him. That warmed Althea's heart. The kid wasn't beaten yet, Althea noted as Liz turned and walked to the door behind her. It shut with a slam.

"Kids," Kline muttered, and lit another cigarette.

"Yeah." Althea smiled sympathetically. "Is she your sister?"

Kline choked on the smoke, but then he grinned. "Right. Yeah, she's my sister. So, you wanted to use the phone?"

"Oh, yes." Setting the mug of coffee aside, Althea rose. "I appreciate it. My friends'll be getting worried about me soon."

"There it is." He gestured. "Help yourself."

"Thanks." But when she picked up the receiver, there was no dial tone. "Gee, I think it's dead."

Kline swore and strode over, pulling a thin L-shaped tool from his pocket. "Forgot. I, ah, lock it up at night, so the kid can't use it. She was making all these long-distance calls and running up the bill. You know how girls are."

"Yes." Althea smiled. "I do." When she heard the dial tone, she punched in the number for the local police. "Fran," she said merrily, addressing the dispatcher as they had arranged. "You won't believe what happened. I got lost, my car broke down. If it hadn't been for these terrific guys, I don't know what I'd have done." She laughed, hoping Colt was making his move. "I do *not* always get lost. I hope Bob's up to coming for me."

* * *

While Althea chatted with the police dispatcher, Colt shimmied up a pole to the second floor. With his binoculars, he'd seen everything he needed to see through the expansive glass of the cabin. Althea was holding her own, and Liz was on the second floor.

They'd agreed that if the opportunity presented itself, he would get her out of the house. Out of harm's way. He might have preferred a direct route—straight through Kline and the other jerk in the living room, and on into the big guy doing kitchen duty.

But Liz's safety came first. Once he got her out, he'd be coming back.

With a grunt, he swung himself onto the narrow overhang and clutched at the window ledge. He saw Liz lying on a rumpled bed, her body turned away and curled up protectively. His first urge was to throw up the window and leap inside. Afraid he might frighten her into crying out, he tapped gently on the glass.

She shifted. When he tapped again, she turned wearily over, unfocused eyes gazing into the sunlight. Then she blinked and cautiously pushed herself up from the bed. Hurriedly Colt put a finger to his lips, signaling silence. But it didn't stop the tears. They poured out of her eyes as she rushed to the window.

"Colt!" She shook the window, then laid her cheek against the glass and wept. "I want to go home! Please, please, I want to go home!"

He could barely hear her through the glass. Afraid their voices would carry, he tapped again, waiting until she turned her head to look at him.

"Open the window, baby." He mouthed it carefully, but she only shook her head.

"Nailed shut." Her breath hitched, and she rubbed her fists against her eyes. "They nailed it shut."

"Okay, okay. Look at me. Look." He used hand signals to focus her attention. "A pillow. Get a pillow."

A dim spark glowed in her eyes. He'd seen it before, that cautious return of hope. She moved fast, doing as he instructed.

"Hold it against the glass. Hold it steady, and turn your head. Turn your head away, baby."

He used his elbow to smash the glass, satisfied that the pillow muffled most of the noise. When he'd broken enough to ease his body through, he nudged the pillow aside and swung inside.

She was immediately in his arms, clinging, sobbing. He picked her up, cradled her like a baby. "Shh…Liz. It's going to be all right now. I'm going to take you home."

"I'm sorry. I'm so sorry."

"Don't worry about it. Don't worry about anything." He drew back to look into her eyes. She looked so thin, he thought, so pale. And he had a lot more to ask of her. "Honey, you're going to have to be tough for a little while longer. We're going to get you out, and we have to move fast. Do you have a coat? Shoes?"

She shook her head. "They took them. They took everything so I couldn't run away. I tried, Colt, I swear I did, but—"

"It's all right." He pressed her face to his shoulder again, recognizing bubbling hysteria. "You're not going to think about it now. You're just going to do exactly what I tell you. Okay?"

"Okay. Can we go now? Right now?"

"Right now. Let's wrap you in this blanket." He dragged it off the bed with one hand and did his best to bundle it around her. "Now we're going to have to take a little fall. But if you hang on to me, and stay real loose, real relaxed, it's going to be fine." He carried her to the window, careful to cover her face against the cold and the jagged teeth of broken glass. "If you want to scream, you scream in your head, but not out loud. That's important."

"I won't scream." With her heart hammering, she pressed hard against his chest. "Please, just take me home. I want Mom."

"She wants you, too. So does your old man." He kept talking in the same low, soothing tone as he inched toward the edge. "We're going to call them as soon as we get out of here." He said a quick prayer and jumped.

He knew how to fall, off a building, down stairs, out of a plane. Without the child, he would simply have tucked and rolled. With her, he swiveled his body to take the brunt of the impact, so that he would land on his back and cushion her.

The impact stole his breath, wrenched his shoulder, but he was up almost as soon as he landed, with Liz still cradled against his chest. He sprinted toward the road and was halfway there when he heard the first shot.

Chapter 10

Althea drew out her conversation with the police dispatcher, pausing in her own chatter to take in the information that her backup's E.T.A. was ten minutes. She sincerely hoped Colt had managed to get Liz away from the cabin, but either way, it looked like it was going to go down as smooth as silk.

"Thanks, Fran. I'm looking forward to seeing you and Bob, too. Just let me get some idea of where I am from Harry. I don't have a clue." Beaming a new smile in Harry's direction, Althea cupped a hand over the phone. "Do you have, like, an address or something? Bob's going to come pick me up and take a look at my car."

"No problem." He glanced over as Tidal Wave came in from the kitchen. "Hope you made enough breakfast for our guest," Harry told him. "She's had a rough morning."

"Yeah, there's enough." Tidal Wave turned his hard brown eyes on Althea, narrowed them. "Hey! What the hell is this?"

"Try for some manners," Donner suggested. "There's a lady present."

"Lady, hell! That's a cop. That's Wild Bill's cop."

He made his lunge, but Althea was ready. She'd seen the recognition in his eyes and had already reached for her weapon. There wasn't time to think or to worry about the other two men, as two hundred and sixty pounds of muscle and bulk rammed her.

Her first shot veered wide as she went flying, slamming against an antique table. A collection of snuff bottles crashed, spewing shards of amethyst and aquamarine. She saw stars. Through them, she saw her opponent bearing down on her like a freight train.

Pure instinct had her rolling to the left to avoid

a blow. Tidal Wave was big, but she was quick. Althea scrambled to her knees and gripped her weapon in both hands.

This time her shot was true. She had only an instant to note the spread of blood on his white T-shirt before she leapt to her feet.

Donner was heading for the door, and Kline was swearing as he dragged open a drawer. She saw the glint of chrome.

"Freeze!"

Her order had Donner throwing up his hands and turning into a statue, but Kline whipped out the gun.

"Do it and die," she told him, stepping back so that she could keep both Kline and Donner in sight. "Drop it, Harry, or you're going to be staining the carpet like your friend there."

"Son of a bitch." Teeth set, he tossed the weapon down.

"Good choice. Now, on the floor, facedown, hands behind your head. You, too, Romeo," she told Donner. While they obeyed, she picked up Kline's gun. "You two should know better than to invite a stranger into the house."

Lord, she hurt, Althea realized now that her adrenaline was leveling off. From the top of her

head to the soles of her feet, she was one huge
ache. She hoped Tidal Wave's flying tackle hadn't
dislodged anything vital.

She caught the thin wail of a siren in the distance. "Looks like old Fran told the troops to come
in. Now, in case you don't get the picture, I'm the
law, and you're under arrest."

Althea was calmly reading her prisoners their
rights when Colt burst in, a gun in one hand, a
knife in the other. By her calculations, it had been
roughly three minutes since she'd fired the first
shot. The man moved fast.

She spared him a glance, then finished the procedure. "Cover these idiots, will you, Nightshade?"
she asked as she picked up the dangling receiver.
"Officer Mooney? Yes, this is Lieutenant Grayson.
We'll need an ambulance out here. I have a suspect
down with a chest wound. No, the situation's under
control. Thank you. You were a big help."

She hung up and looked back at Colt. "Liz?"

"She's okay. I told her to wait by the road for the
cops. I heard the shots." His hands were steady. He
could be grateful for that. But his insides were
jelly. "I figured they'd made you."

"You figured right. That one." She jerked her
head toward Tidal Wave. "He must have seen me

with Wild Bill. Why don't you go find us a towel? We'd better try to stop that bleeding."

"The hell with that!" The fury came so suddenly, and so violently, that the two men on the floor quaked. "Your head's cut."

"Yeah?" She touched her fingers to the throbbing ache at her right temple, then studied her blood-smeared fingers in disgust. "Hell. That better not need stitches. I really hate stitches."

"Which one of them hit you?" Colt scanned the three men with icy eyes. "Which one?"

"The one I shot. The one who's currently bleeding to death. Now get me a towel, and we'll see if we can have him live long enough to go to trial." When he didn't respond, she stepped between him and the wounded man. Colt's intentions were clear as crystal. "Don't pull this crap on me, Nightshade. I'm not a damsel in distress, and white knights annoy the hell out of me. Got it?"

"Yeah." He sucked in his breath. There were too many emotions ripping through him. None of them could change the situation. "Yeah, I got it, Lieutenant."

He turned away to do as she'd asked. After all, he thought, she could handle the situation. She could handle anything.

* * *

It wasn't until they were in the plane again that he began to calm. He had to at least pretend to be calm for Liz's sake. She'd clung to him, begging him not to send her back with the police, to stay with her. So he'd agreed to fly back with Liz in the copilot's seat and Althea in the jump seat behind.

Looking lost in his coat, Liz stared through the windscreen. No matter how Colt had tried to bundle her up, she continued to shiver. When they leveled off, heading east, the tears began to flow. They fell fast, hot, down her cheeks. Her shoulders shook violently, but she made no sound. No sound at all.

"Come on, baby." Helpless, Colt reached out to take her hand. "Everything's all right now. Nobody's going to hurt you now."

But the silent tears continued.

Saying nothing, Althea rose. She came forward, calmly unstrapped Liz. Communicating by touch, Althea urged Liz to shift, then took her place in the chair. Then she gathered the girl on her lap, cradled her head on her shoulder. Enfolded her grief.

"Don't hold back," she murmured.

Almost at once, Liz's sobs echoed through the cabin. The pain in them cut at Althea's heart as she rocked the girl and held her close. Devastated by the weeping, Colt lifted a hand to brush it down Liz's tangled hair. But she only curled closer to Althea at the touch.

He dropped his hand and concentrated on the sky.

It was Althea's gentle insistence that convinced Liz it would be wise to go to the hospital first. She wanted to go home, she said over and over again. And over and over again, Althea patiently reminded Liz that her parents were already on their way to Denver.

"I know it's hard." Althea kept her arm tight around Liz's shoulders. "And I know it's scary, but the doctor needs to check you out."

"I don't want him to touch me."

"I know." How well she knew. "But he's a she." Althea smiled, rubbing her hand down Liz's arm. "She won't hurt you."

"It'll be over real quick," Colt assured her. He fought to keep his easy smile in place. What he wanted to do was scream. Kick something. Kill someone.

"Okay." Liz glanced warily toward the examining room again. "Please…" She pressed her lips together and looked pleadingly at Althea.

"Would you like me to go in with you? Stay with you?" At Liz's nod, she drew the girl closer. "Sure, no problem. Colt, why don't you go find a soft-drink machine, maybe a candy bar?" She smiled down at Liz. "I could sure use some chocolate. How about you?"

"Yeah." Liz drew in a shaky breath. "I guess."

"We'll be back in a few minutes," Althea told Colt. He could read nothing in her eyes. Feeling useless, he strode down the corridor.

Inside the examining room, Althea helped Liz exchange her tattered clothes for a hospital gown. She noted the bruises on the girl's flesh, but made no comment. They would need an official statement from Liz, but it could wait a little longer.

"This is Dr. Mailer," she explained as the young doctor with the soft eyes approached the table.

"Hello, Liz." Dr. Mailer didn't offer her hand, or touch her patient in any way. She specialized in trauma patients, and she understood the terrors of rape victims. "I'm going to need to ask you some questions, and to run some tests. If there's anything you want to ask me, you go ahead. And if you want me to stop, to wait a while, you just say so. Okay?"

"All right." Liz lay back and focused on the ceiling. But her hand remained tight around Althea's.

Althea had requested Dr. Mailer because she knew the woman's reputation. As the examination progressed, she was more than satisfied that it was well deserved. The doctor was gentle, kind and efficient. It seemed she instinctively knew when to stop, to give Liz a chance to regroup, and when to continue.

"We're all done." Dr. Mailer stripped off her gloves and smiled. "I just want you to rest in here for a little while, and I'm going to have a prescription for you before you leave."

"I don't have to stay here, do I?"

"No." Dr. Mailer closed a hand over Liz's. "You did fine. When your parents get here, we'll talk again. Why don't I see about getting you something to eat?"

As she left, Dr. Mailer sent Althea a look that clearly stated that they, too, would talk later.

"You did do fine," Althea said, helping Liz to sit up. "Do you want me to go see if Colt found that candy bar? I don't imagine that's the sort of food Dr. Mailer had in mind, so we'll have to sneak it while we can."

"I don't want to be alone here."

"Okay." Althea took her brush from her purse and began to untangle Liz's hair. "Let me know if I'm pulling."

"When I saw you downstairs—at the cabin—I thought you were another of the women they brought up. That it was going to happen again." Liz squeezed her eyes shut. Tears spilled through her lashes. "That they were going to make me do those things again."

"I'm sorry. There wasn't any way to let you know I was there to help you."

"And when I saw Colt at the window, I thought it was a dream. I kept dreaming somebody would come, but no one did. I was afraid Mom and Dad just didn't care."

"Honey, your parents have been trying to find you all along." She tipped Liz's chin upward. "They've been so worried. That's why they sent Colt. And I can tell you he loves you, too. You can't imagine the stuff he's bullied me into doing so he could find you."

Liz tried to smile, but it quivered and fell. "But they don't know about— Maybe they won't love me after they find out…everything."

"No." Althea's fingers firmed on Liz's chin. "It'll upset them, and it will hurt them, and it'll be hard, really hard, for them. That's because they do love you. Nothing that happened is going to change that."

"I—I can't do anything but cry."

"Then that's all you have to do, for now."

Liz swiped a shaky hand across her cheeks. "It was my fault I ran away."

"It was your fault you ran away," Althea agreed. "That's all that was your fault."

Liz jerked her head away. The tears gushed out again as she stared at the tiles on the floor. "You don't understand how it feels. You don't know what it's like. How awful it is. How humiliating."

"You're wrong." Gently, firmly, Althea cupped Liz's face again, lifting it until their eyes met. "I do understand. I understand exactly."

"You?" Air shuddered out between Liz's lips. "It happened to you?"

"When I was just about your age. And I felt as though someone had carved something out of me that I'd never get back again. I thought I'd never get clean again, be whole again. Be me again. And I cried for a long, long time, because there didn't seem to be anything else I could do."

Liz accepted the tissue Althea pressed into her hand. "I kept telling myself it wasn't me. It wasn't really me. But I was so scared. It's over. Colt keeps saying it's over now, but it hurts."

"I know." Althea cradled Liz in her arms again. "It hurts more than anything else can, and it's going to hurt for a while. But you're not alone. You have to keep remembering you're not alone. You have your family, your friends. You have Colt. And you can talk to me whenever you need to."

Liz sniffled, rested her cheek against Althea's heart. "What did you do? After. What did you do?"

"I survived," Althea murmured, staring blankly over Liz's head. "And so will you."

Colt stood in the doorway of the examining room, his arms piled high with cans of soda and candy bars. If he'd felt useless before, he now felt unbearably helpless.

There was no place for him here, no way for him to intrude on this woman pain. His first and only reaction was rage. But where to channel it? He turned away to dump the cans and candy onto a table in the waiting room. If he couldn't comfort either of them, couldn't stop what had already happened, then what could he do?

He scrubbed his hands over his face and tried to clear his mind. Even as he dropped them, he saw Liz's parents dashing from the elevator.

This, at least, he could do. He strode to meet them.

Inside the examining room, Althea finished tidying Liz's hair. "Do you want to get dressed?"

Liz managed what passed for a smile. "I don't ever want to put those clothes on again."

"Good point. Well, maybe I can scrounge up—" She turned at a flurry of movement in the doorway. She saw a pale woman and a haggard man, both with red-rimmed eyes.

"Oh, baby! Oh, Liz!" The woman raced forward first, with the man right on her heels.

"Mom!" Liz was sobbing again even as she threw open her arms. "Mom!"

Althea stepped aside as parents and child were reunited, with tears and desperate embraces. When she spotted Colt in the doorway, she moved to him. "You'd better stay with them. I'll tell Dr. Mailer they're here before I go."

"Where are you going?"

She slid her purse back on her shoulder. "To file my report."

She did just that before she went home to indulge in that long, steamy bath. She soaked until her body was numb. Giving in to exhaustion, both physical and emotional, she fell into bed naked and slept dreamlessly until the battering on her door awoke her.

Groggy, she fumbled for her robe, belting it as

she walked to the door. She scowled at Colt through the peephole, then yanked the door open.

"Give me one good reason why I shouldn't book you for disturbing the peace. My peace."

He held out a flat, square box. "I brought you pizza."

She blew out a breath, then drew one in—as well as the rich scent of cheese and spice. "That might get you off. I guess you want to come in with it."

"That was the idea."

"Well, come on, then." With that dubious invitation, she walked away to fetch plates and napkins. "How's Liz holding up?"

"Surprisingly well. Marleen and Frank are as solid as they come."

"They'll have to be." She came back to set the plates on the table. "I hope they understand they're all going to need counseling."

"They've already talked to Dr. Mailer about it. She's going to help them find a good therapist back home." Trying to choose his words properly, he took his time sliding pizza onto the plates. "The first thing I want to do is thank you. And don't brush me off, Thea. I'd really like to get this out."

"All right, then." She sat, picked up a slice. "Get it out."

"I'm not just talking about the official cooperation, the way you helped me find her and get her out. I owe you big for that, but that's professional. You got anything to drink with this?"

"There's some burgundy in the kitchen."

"I'll get it," he said as she started to rise.

Althea shrugged and went back to eating. "Suit yourself." She was working on her second slice when Colt came back with a bottle and two glasses. "I guess I was too tired to realize I was starving."

"Then I don't have to apologize for waking you up." He filled both glasses, but didn't drink. "The other thing I have to thank you for is the way you were with Liz. I figured getting her out was enough—playing that white knight you said irritates you so much." He looked up, met her eyes. There was a new understanding in them, and a weariness she hadn't seen before. "It wasn't. Telling her it was all right, that it was over—that wasn't enough, either. She needed you."

"She needed a woman."

"You are that. I know it's a lot to expect—over and above, so to speak—but she asked about you a couple of times after you left." He toyed with the stem of his glass. "They're going to be staying in town at least for another day, until Dr. Mailer has some of the results in. I was hoping you could talk to Liz again."

"You don't have to ask me that, Colt." She reached out for his hand. "I got involved, too."

"So did I, Thea." He turned their joined hands over, brought them to his lips. "I'm in love with you. Big-time. No, don't pull away from me." He tightened his grip before she could. "I've never said that to another woman. I used alternate terms." He smiled a little. "I'm crazy about you, you're special to me, that kind of thing. But I never used *love,* not until you."

She believed him. What was more frightening, she wanted to believe him. Tread carefully, she reminded herself. One step at a time. "Listen, Colt, the two of us have been on a roller coaster since we met—and that's only been a short while. Things, emotions, get blown out of proportion on roller coasters. Why don't we slow this down some?"

He could feel her nerves jittering, but he couldn't be amused by them this time. "I had to accept that I couldn't change what had happened to Liz. That was hard. I can't change what I feel for you. Accepting that's easy."

"I'm not sure what you want from me, Colt, and I don't think I can give it to you."

"Because of what happened to you before. Because of what I heard you telling Liz in the examining room."

She withdrew instantly and completely. "That was between Liz and me," she said coldly. "And it's none of your business."

It was exactly the reaction he'd expected, the one he'd prepared for. "We both know that's not true. But we'll talk about it when you're ready." Knowing the value of keeping an opponent off balance, he picked up his wine. "You know they're giving Scott a fifty-fifty chance of making it."

"I know." She watched him warily. "I called the hospital before I went to bed. Boyd's handling the interrogation of Kline and Donner for now."

"Can't wait to get at them, can you?"

"No." She smiled again. "I can't."

"You know, I heard those shots, and it stopped my heart." Feeling more relaxed, he bit into his pizza. "I come tearing back, ready to kick butt, crash through the door like the cavalry, and what do I see?" He shook his head and tapped her glass with his. "There you are, blood running down your face…" He paused to touch a gentle finger to the bandage at her temple. "A gun in each hand. There's a three-hundred-pound hulk bleeding at your feet, and two others facedown with their hands behind their heads. You're just standing there, looking like Diana after the hunt, and reciting Miranda. I have to say, I felt pretty superfluous."

"You did okay, Nightshade." She let out a small, defeated breath. "And I guess you deserve to know that I was awfully glad to see you. You looked like Jim Bowie at the Alamo."

"He lost."

She gave in and leaned forward to kiss him. "You didn't."

"We didn't," he corrected, pleased that her mouth had been soft, relaxed and friendly. "I brought you a present."

"Oh, yeah?" Because the dangerous moment seemed to have passed, her lips curved and she kissed him again. "Gimme."

He reached behind himself for his coat, dug into the pocket. Taking out a small paper bag, he tossed it into her lap.

"Aw, and you wrapped it so nice." Chuckling, she dipped into the bag. And pulled out a lacy bra and panties, in sheer midnight blue. Her chuckle turned into a rich appreciative laugh.

"I pay my debts," he informed her. "Since I figured you probably had a supply of the white kind, I picked out something a little different." He reached over to feel the silk and lace. "Maybe you'll try them on."

"Eventually." But she knew what she wanted now. What she needed now. And she rose to take it. She combed her fingers through his hair, tugging so that his face lifted and his mouth met hers. "Maybe you'll come to bed with me."

"Absolutely." He skimmed his hands up her hips, keeping his mouth joined to hers as he stood to gather her close. "I thought you'd never ask."

"I didn't want the pizza to get cold."

He slipped a finger down the center of her body to toy with the belt of her robe. "Still hungry?"

She tugged his shirt out of his jeans. "Now that you mention it." Then she laughed as he swung her up into his arms. "What's this for?"

"I decided to sweep you off your feet. For now." He started toward the bedroom, deciding she was in for another surprise.

The spread was turned back, but the plain white sheets were barely disturbed from her nap. Colt laid her down, following her onto the bed as he skimmed light, teasing kisses over her face.

Her fingers were busy undoing his buttons. She knew what it would be like, and was prepared— eager—for the storm and the fire and the fast flood of sensations. When her hands pushed away cotton and encountered warm, firm flesh, she gave a low, satisfied moan.

He continued to kiss her, nibbling, nuzzling, as she hastily stripped off his clothes. There was a frantic energy burning in her that promised the wild, the frenzied. Each time desire stabbed through him, he absorbed the shock and kept his pace easy.

Eager, edgy, Althea turned her mouth to his and arched against him. "I want you."

He hadn't realized that three breathy words could make the blood swim in his head. But it would be too easy to take what she offered, too easy to lose what she held back. "I know. I can taste it."

He dipped his mouth to hers again, drawing out the kiss with such trembling tenderness that she groaned again. The hand that had been fisted tight against his bare shoulder went lax.

"And I want you," he murmured, levering back

to stare down at her. "All of you." Fascinated, he drew his fingers through her hair, spreading it out until it lay flaming against the white sheet. Then he lowered his head again, gently, so gently, to kiss the bandage at her temple.

Emotion curled inside her like a spiked fist. "Colt—"

"Shh…I just want to look."

And look he did, while he traced her face with a fingertip, rubbed her lower lip with his thumb, then trailed it down to her jawline, skimmed over the pulse that fluttered in her throat.

"The sun's going down," he said quietly. "The light does incredible things to your face, your eyes. Just now they're gold, with darker, brandy-colored specks sprinkled through them. I've never seen eyes like yours. You look like a painting." He brushed his thumb over her collarbone. "But I can touch you, feel you tremble, know you're real."

She lifted a hand, wanting to drag him back to her, to make the ache go away. "I don't need words."

"Sure you do." He smiled a little, turning his face into her palm. "Maybe I haven't found the right ones, but you need them." He started to press his lips to her wrist, and then he noticed the faint smudge of bruises. And remembered.

His brows drew together when he straddled her and took both of her hands. He examined her wrists carefully before looking down at her again. "I did this."

Sweet God, she thought, there had to be a way to stop this terrible trembling. "It doesn't matter. You were upset. Make love with me."

"I don't like knowing I hurt you in anger, or that I'm liable to do it again eventually." Very carefully, he touched his lips to each of her wrists, and felt her pulse scramble. "You make it too easy to forget how soft you are, Althea." The sleeves of her robe slithered down her arms as he skimmed his lips to her elbow. "How small. How incredibly perfect you are. I'll have to show you."

He cupped a hand under her head, lifting her so that her hair tumbled back, her face tilted up. Then his mouth was on hers again, savoring a deep, dreamy kiss that left her weak. He felt her give, felt yet another layer dissolve. Her arms linked around his neck; her muscles quivered.

What was he doing to her? She only knew she couldn't think, couldn't resist. She'd been prepared for need, and he'd given her tenderness.

What defense could there be against passion wrapped so softly in sweetness? His mouth was gentle, enchanting her even as it seduced.

She wanted to tell him that seduction was unnecessary, but, oh, it felt glorious to surrender to the secrets he unearthed with that quietly devastating mouth and those slow, easy hands.

The last rays of the sun slanted across her eyes as he eased her back so that he could trail his lips down her throat. She heard the whisper of her robe as he slipped it down to bare her shoulder, to free it for lazy, openmouthed kisses and the moist trail of his tongue.

He could feel it the instant she let herself go. The warmth of triumph surged through him as her hands, as gentle as his, began to caress. He resisted the urge to quicken his pace, and let his hands explore her, over the robe, under it, then over again, as her body melted like warm wax.

All the while, he watched her face, aroused by each flicker of emotion, lured by the way her breath would catch, then rush through her lips at his touch. He could have sworn he felt her float as he slipped the robe away.

Then her eyes opened, dark and heavy. He understood that, though she had surrendered, she would not be passive. Her hands were as thorough as his, seeking, touching, possessing, with that unbearable tenderness.

Until he was as seduced as she.

Soft, breathy moans. Quiet secrets told in murmurs. Long, lingering caresses. The sunlight faded to dusk, and dusk to that deepening of night. There was need, but no frantic rush to sate it. There was pleasure, and the dreamy desire to prolong it.

Indulgence. Tonight there was only indulgence.

He touched, she trembled. She tasted, he shuddered.

When at last he slipped into her, she smiled and gathered him close. The rhythm they set was patient, loving, and as true as music. They climbed together, steadily, beautifully, until his gasp echoed hers. And then they floated back to earth.

She lay a long time in silence, dazed by what had happened. He had given her something, and she had given freely in return. It couldn't be taken back. She wondered what steps could be taken to protect herself now that she had fallen in love.

For the first time. For the only time.

Perhaps it would pass. A part of her cringed at the thought of losing what she'd just found. No matter how firmly she reminded herself that her life was precisely the way she wanted it, she couldn't bring herself to think too deeply about what it would be like without him.

And yet she had no choice. He would leave. And she would survive.

"You're thinking again." He rolled onto his back, hooking an arm around her to gather her close. "I can almost hear your brain humming." Outrageously content, he kissed her hair, closed his eyes. "Tell me the first thing that pops into your mind."

"What? I don't—"

"No, no, don't analyze. This is a test. The first thing, Thea. Now."

"I was wondering when you were going back," she heard herself say. "To Wyoming."

"Ah." He smiled—smugly. "I like knowing I'm the first thing on your mind."

"Don't get cocky, Nightshade."

"Okay. I haven't made any firm plans. I have some loose ends to tie up first."

"Such as?"

"You, for starters. We haven't set the date."

"Colt…"

He grinned again. Maybe it was wishful thinking, but he thought he'd heard exasperation in her tone instead of annoyance. "I'm still shooting for New Year's Eve—I guess I've gotten sentimental—but we've got time to hash that out. Then there's the fact that I haven't finished what I came here to do."

That brought her head up. "What do you mean? You found Liz."

"It's not enough." His eyes glowed in the shadows. "We don't have the head man. It's not finished until we do."

"That's for me and the department to worry about. Personal vendettas have no place here."

"I didn't say it was a vendetta." Though it was. "I intend to finish this, Althea. I'd like to keep working with you on this."

"And if I say no?"

He twirled her hair around his finger. "I'll do my best to change your mind. Maybe you haven't noticed, but I can be tenacious."

"I've noticed," she muttered. But there was a part of her that glowed at the idea that their partnership wasn't at an end. "I suppose I can give you a few more days."

"Good." He shifted her so that he could run a hand down her side to her hips. "Does the deal include a few more nights?"

"I suppose it could." Her smile flashed wickedly. "If you make it worth my while."

"Oh, I will." He lowered his head. "That's a promise."

Chapter 11

With the scream still tearing at her throat, Althea shot up in bed. Blind with terror and rage, she fought the arms that wound around her, struggling wildly against the hold while she sucked in the air to scream again. She could feel his hands on her, feel them groping at her, hot, hurtful. But this time…God, please, this time…

"Althea." Colt shook her, hard, forcing his voice to remain calm and firm, though his heart was hammering against his ribs in fast, hard blows. "Althea, wake up. You're dreaming. Pull out of it."

She clawed her way through the slippery edges

of the dream, still fighting him, still dragging in air. Reality was a dim light through the murky depths of the nightmare. With a final burst of effort, she grasped at it, and at Colt.

"Okay, okay…" Still shaken by the sound of the scream that had awakened him, he rocked her, holding her close to warm her body, which was chill with clammy sweat. "Okay, baby. Just hold on to me."

"Oh, God…" Her breath came out in a long, shaky sob as she buried her face against his shoulder. Her hands fisted impotently at his back. "Oh, God… Oh, God…"

"It's okay now." He continued to stroke and soothe, growing concerned when her hold on him increased. "I'm right here. You were dreaming, that's all. You were only dreaming."

She'd fought her way out of the dream, but the fear had come back with her, and it was too huge to allow for shame. So she clung, shivering, trying to absorb some portion of the strength she felt in him.

"Just give me a minute. I'll be all right in a minute." The shaking would stop, she told herself. The tears would dry. The fear would ebb. "I'm sorry." But it wasn't stopping. Instinctively she turned her face into his throat for comfort. "God, I'm sorry."

"Just relax." She was quivering like a bird, he thought, and she felt as frail as one. "Do you want me to turn on the light?"

"No." She pressed her lips together, hoping to stop the trembling in her voice. She didn't want the light. Didn't want him to see her until she'd managed to compose herself. "No. Let me get some water. I'll be fine."

"I'll get it." He brushed the hair from her face, and was shaken all over again to find it wet with tears. "I'll be right back."

She brought her knees up close to her chest when he left her. Control, she ordered herself, but dropped her head onto her knees. While she listened to water striking glass, watched the splinter of light spill through the crack around the bathroom door, she took long, even breaths.

"Sorry, Nightshade," she said when he came back with the water. "I guess I woke you up."

"I guess you did." Her voice was steadier, he noted. But her hands weren't. He cupped his around hers and lifted the glass to her lips. "Must have been a bad one."

The water eased her dry throat. "Must have been. Thanks." She pushed the glass back into his hands, embarrassed that she couldn't hold it herself.

Colt set the glass on the night table before easing down on the bed beside her. "Tell me."

She moved her shoulders dismissively. "Chalk it up to a rough day and pizza."

Very firmly, very gently, he took her face in his hands. The light he'd left on in the bathroom sent out a dim glow. In it he could see how pale she was.

"No. I'm not going to brush this off, Thea. You're not going to brush me off. You were screaming." She tried to turn her head away, but he wouldn't permit it. "You're still shaking. I can be every bit as stubborn as you, and right now I think I have the advantage."

"I had a nightmare." She wanted to snap at him, but couldn't find the strength. "People have nightmares."

"How often do you have this one?"

"Never." She lifted a weary hand and dragged it through her hair. "Not in years. I don't know what brought it on."

He thought he did. And unless he was very much mistaken, he thought she did, as well. "Do you have a shirt, a nightgown or something? You're cold."

"I'll get one."

"Just tell me where." Her quick, annoyed sigh did quite a bit toward easing his mind.

"Top drawer of the dresser. Left-hand side."

He rose, and opening the drawer grabbed the first thing that came to hand. Before he tugged it over her head, he examined the oversize man's undershirt. "Nice lingerie you have, Lieutenant."

"It does the job."

He smoothed it down over her, tucked pillows behind her, as fussy as a mother with a colicky infant.

She scowled at him. "I don't like being pampered."

"You'll live through it."

When he was satisfied he'd made her as comfortable as possible, he tugged on his jeans. They were going to talk, he decided, and sat beside her again. Whether she wanted to or not. He took her hand, waited until they were eye-to-eye.

"The nightmare. It was about when you were raped, wasn't it?" Her fingers went rigid in his. "I told you I heard you talking to Liz."

She ordered her fingers to relax, willed them to, but they remained stiff and cold. "It was a long time ago. It doesn't apply now."

"It does when it wakes you up screaming. It brought it all back," he continued quietly. "What happened to Liz, seeing her through it."

"All right. So what?"

"Trust me, Althea." He said it quietly, his eyes on hers. "Let me help."

"It hurts," she heard herself say. Then she shut her eyes. It was the first time she had admitted that to anyone. "Not all the time. Not even most of the time. It just sneaks up now and then and slices at you."

"I want to understand." He brought her hand to his lips. When she didn't pull away, he left it there. "Talk, talk to me."

She didn't know where to begin. It seemed safest to start at the beginning. Letting her head rest against the pillows, she closed her eyes again.

"My father drank, and when he drank, he got drunk, and when he got drunk, he got mean. He had big hands." She curled hers into fists, then relaxed them. "He used them on my mother, on me. My earliest memory is of those hands, the anger in them that I couldn't understand, and couldn't fight. I don't remember him very well. He tangled with somebody meaner one night and ended up dead. I was six."

She opened her eyes again, realizing that keeping them closed was just another way of hiding. "Once he was gone, my mother decided to take up where he'd left off—in the bottle. She didn't hit it as hard as he did, but she was more consistent."

He could only wonder how the people she'd described could have created anything as beautiful or as true as the woman beside him. "Did you have anyone else?"

"I had grandparents, on my mother's side. I don't know where they lived. I never met them. They hadn't had anything to do with her since she'd run off with my father."

"But did they know about you?"

"If they did, they didn't care."

He said nothing, trying to comprehend it. But he couldn't, simply couldn't understand family not caring. "Okay. What did you do?"

"When you're a child, you do nothing," she said flatly. "You're at the mercy of adults, and the reality is, a great many adults have no mercy." She paused a moment to pick up the threads of the story. "When I was about eight, she went out—she went out a lot—but this time she didn't come home. A couple of days later, a neighbor called Social Services. They scooped me up into the system."

She reached for the water again. This time her hands didn't shake. "It's a long, typical story."

"I want to hear it."

"They placed me in a foster home." She sipped her water. There wasn't any point in telling him how frightened, how lost, she'd been. The facts were enough. "It was okay. Decent. Then they found her, slapped her wrists a couple of times, told her to clean up her act, and gave me back."

"Why in the hell did they do that?"

"Things were different back then. The court believed the best place for a kid was with her mother. Anyway, she didn't stay dry for long, and the cycle started all over again. I ran away a few times, they dragged me back. More foster homes. They don't leave you in any one too long, especially when you're recalcitrant. And I'd developed my own mean streak by that time."

"Small wonder."

"I bounced around in the system. Social workers, court hearings, school counselors. All overburdened. My mother hooked up with another guy and finally took off for good. Mexico, I think. In any case, she didn't come back. I was twelve, thirteen. I hated not being able to say where I wanted to go, where I wanted to be. I took off every chance I got. So they labeled me a j.d.—juvenile delinquent— and they put me in a girls' home, which was one step up from reform school." Her lips twisted into a dry smile. "That put the fear of God into me. It was rough, as close to prison as I ever want to be. So I straightened up, put on my best behavior. Eventually they placed me in foster care again."

She drained the glass and set it aside. She knew her hands wouldn't be steady for long. "I was scared that if I didn't make it work this time, they'd put me back until I was eighteen. So I took a real shot at it. They were a nice couple, naive, maybe, but nice, good intentions. They wanted to do something to right society's ills. She was PTA president, and they went to protest rallies against nuclear power plants. They talked about adopting a Vietnamese orphan. I guess I smirked at them behind their backs sometimes, but I really liked them. They were kind to me."

She took a moment, and he said nothing, waiting for her to build to the next stage. "They gave me boundaries, good ones, and they treated me fairly. There was one drawback. They had a son. He was seventeen, captain of the football team, homecoming king, A student. The apple of their eye. A real company man."

"Company man?"

"You know, the kind who's all slick and polished on the outside, he's got a terrific rap, lots of charm, lots of angles. And underneath, he's slime. You can't get to the slime because you keep slipping on all that polish, but it's there." Her eyes glinted at the memory. "I could see it. I hated the way he looked at me when they weren't watching." Her breath was coming quicker now, but her voice was still controlled. "Like I was a piece of meat he was sizing up, getting ready to grill. They couldn't see it. All they saw was this perfect child who never gave them a moment's grief. And one night, when they were out, he came home from a date. God."

When she covered her face with her hands, Colt gathered her close. "It's all right, Thea. That's enough."

"No." She shook her head violently, pushed back. She'd gone this far. She'd finish it. "He was angry. I suppose his girl hadn't surrendered to his many charms. He came into my room. When I told him to get out, he just laughed and reminded me it was his house, and that I was only there because his parents felt sorry for me. Of course, he was right."

"No. No, he wasn't."

"He was right about that," Althea insisted. "Not

about the rest, but about that. And he unzipped his pants. I ran for the door, but he threw me back on the bed. I hit my head pretty hard on the wall. I remember being dizzy for a minute, and hearing him telling me that he knew girls like me usually charged for it, but that I should be flattered that he was going to give me a thrill. He got on the bed. I slapped him, I swore at him. He backhanded me, and pinned me. And I started to scream. I kept screaming and screaming while he raped me. When he was finished, I wasn't screaming anymore. I was just crying. He got off the bed, and zipped up his pants. He warned me that if I told anyone he'd deny it. And who were they going to believe, someone like him, or someone like me? He was blood, so there was no contest. And he could always get five of his buddies to say that I'd been willing with all of them. Then they'd just put me back in the home.

"So I didn't say anything, because there was nothing to say and no one to say it to. He raped me twice more over the next month, before I got the nerve to run away again. Of course, they caught me. Maybe I'd wanted them to that time. I stayed in the home until I was eighteen. And when I got out, I knew no one was ever going to have that kind of control over me again. No one was ever going to make me feel like I was nothing ever again."

Unsure what to do, Colt reached up tentatively to brush a tear from her cheek. "You made your life into something, Althea."

"I made it into mine." She let out a breath, then briskly rubbed the tears from her cheeks. "I don't like to dwell on before, Colt."

"But it's there."

"It's there," she agreed. "Trying to make it go away only brings it closer to the surface. I learned that, too. Once you accept it's simply a part of what makes you what you are, it doesn't become as vital. It didn't make me hate men, it didn't make me hate myself. It did make me understand what it is to be a victim."

He wanted to gather her close, but was afraid she might not want to be touched. "I wish I could make the hurt go away."

"Old scars," she murmured. "They only ache at odd moments." She sensed his withdrawal, and felt the ache spread. "I'm the same person I was before I told you. The trouble is, after people hear a story like that, they change."

"I haven't changed." He started to touch her, drew back. "Damn it, Thea, I don't know what to say to you. What to do for you." Rising, he paced away from the bed. "I could make you some tea."

She nearly laughed. "Nightshade's cure-all? No thanks."

"What do you want?" he demanded. "Just tell me."

"Why don't you tell me what you want?"

"What I want." He strode to the window, whirled back. "I want to go back to when you were fifteen and kick that bastard's face in. I want to hurt him a hundred times worse than he hurt you. Then I want to go back further and break your father's legs, and I want to kick your mother's butt while I'm at it."

"Well, you can't," she said coolly. "Pick something else."

"I want to hold you!" he shouted, jamming his fists into his pockets. "And I'm afraid to touch you!"

"I don't want your tea, and I don't want your sympathy. So if that's all you have to offer, you might as well leave."

"Is that what you want?"

"What I want is to be accepted for who and what I am. Not to be tiptoed around like an invalid because I survived rape and abuse."

He started to snap back at her, then stopped

himself. He wasn't thinking of her, he realized, but of his own rage, his own impotence, his own pain. Slowly he walked back to the bed and sat beside her. Her eyes were still wet; he could see them gleaming against the shadows. He slipped his arms around her, gently drew her close until her head rested on his shoulder.

"I'm not going anywhere," he murmured. "Okay?"

She sighed, settled. "Okay."

Althea awakened at sunrise with a dull headache. She knew instantly that Colt was no longer beside her. Wearily she rolled onto her back and rubbed her swollen eyes.

What had she expected? she asked herself. No man would be comfortable around a woman after hearing a story like the one she'd told him. And why in God's name had she dumped out her past that way? How could she have trusted him with pieces of herself that she'd never given anyone before?

Even Boyd, the person she considered her closest friend, knew only about the foster homes. As for the rest, she'd buried it—until last night.

She didn't doubt that her tie to Liz had unlocked

the door and let the nightmare back in. But she should have been able to handle it, to hold back, to safeguard her privacy. The fact that she hadn't could mean only one thing.

Indulging in a sigh, Althea pushed herself up and rested her brow on her knees.

She was in love with Colt. Ridiculous as it was, she had to face the truth. And, just as she'd always suspected, love made you stupid, vulnerable and unhappy.

There ought to be a pill, she mused. A serum she could take. Like an antidote for snakebite.

The sound of footsteps had her whipping her head up. Her eyes widened when Colt came to the doorway carrying a tray.

He had a split second to read her reaction before she closed it off. She'd thought he'd taken a hike, he realized grimly. He was going to have to show the lady that he was sticking, no matter how hard she tried to shake him off.

"Morning, Lieutenant. I figured you'd planned on a full day."

"You figured right." Cautious, she watched as he crossed to the bed, waited until he'd set the tray at her feet. "What's the occasion?" she asked, gesturing toward the plates of French toast.

"I owe you a breakfast. Remember?"

"Yeah." Her gaze shifted from the plates to his face. Love still made her feel stupid, it still made her feel vulnerable, but it no longer made her unhappy. "You're a regular whiz in the kitchen."

"We all have our talents." He sat cross-legged on the other side of the tray and dug in. "I figure—" he chewed, swallowed "—after we're married, I can handle the meals, you can handle the laundry."

She ignored the quick sprint of panic and sampled her first bite. "You ought to see someone about this obsessive fantasy life of yours, Nightshade."

"My mother's dying to meet you." He grinned when Althea's fork clattered against her plate. "She and Dad send their best."

"You—" Words failed her.

"She and my father know Liz. I called to relieve their minds, and I told them about you." Smiling, he brushed her hair back from her shoulders. He hadn't known a woman could look so sexy in a man's undershirt. "She's for a spring wedding— you know, all that June-bride stuff. But I told her I wasn't waiting that long."

"You're out of your mind."

"Maybe." His grin faded. "But I'm in yours,

Thea. I'm in there real good, and I'm not getting out."

He was right about that, but it didn't change the bottom line. She was not walking down the aisle and saying 'I do.' That was that.

"Listen, Colt." Try reason, she thought. "I'm very fond of you, but—"

"You're what?" His mouth quirked again. "You're what of me?"

"Fond," she spit out, infuriated by the gleam of good humor in his eyes.

"Euphemisms." Affectionately he patted her hand, shook his head. "You disappoint me, I had you pegged as a straight shooter."

Forget reason. "Just shut up and let me eat."

He obliged her, because it gave him time to think, and to study her. She was still a bit pale, he mused. And her eyes were swollen from the bout of tears during the night. But she wouldn't let herself be fragile. He had to admire her unceasing supply of strength. She didn't want sympathy, he remembered, she wanted understanding. She would just have to learn to accept both from him.

She'd accepted his comfort the night before. Whether she knew it or not, she'd already come to rely on him. He wasn't about to let her down.

"How's the coffee?"

"Good." And because it was, because the meal he'd prepared had already conquered her headache, she relented. "Thanks."

"My pleasure." He leaned forward, touched his mouth to hers. "I don't suppose I could interest you in an after-breakfast tussle."

She smiled now, fully, easily. "I'll have to take a rain check." But she spread a hand over his chest and kissed him again. Her fingers closed over his medal. "Why do you wear this?"

"My grandmother gave it to me. She said that when a man was determined not to settle down in one place, he should have someone looking out for him. It's worked pretty well so far." He set the tray on the floor, then scooped Althea into his arms.

"Nightshade, I said—"

"I know, I know." He hitched her up more comfortably. "But I had this idea that if we had that tussle in the shower, we could stay pretty much on schedule."

She laughed, nipped at his shoulder. "I'm a firm believer in time management."

She had more than a full day to fit into twenty-four hours. There was a mountain of paperwork waiting for her, and she needed to talk to Boyd about his interrogation of Donner and Kline before she met with them herself. She wanted, for personal, as well as professional, reasons, to interview Liz again.

She sat down and began efficiently chipping away at the mountain.

Cilla knocked on the open door. "Excuse me, Lieutenant. Got a minute?"

"For the captain's wife," she said, smiling and gesturing Cilla inside, "I've got a minute and a half. What are you doing down here?"

"Boyd filled me in." Cilla leaned down, peered close and, as a woman would, saw through the meticulously applied cosmetics to the signs of a difficult night. "Are you all right?"

"I'm fine. I have decided that anyone who camps out on purpose needs immediate psychiatric help, but it was an experience."

"You should try it with three kids."

"No," Althea said definitely. "No, I shouldn't."

With a laugh, Cilla rested a hip against the edge of the desk. "I'm so glad you and Colt found the girl. How's she doing?"

"It'll be rough for a while, but she'll come through."

"Those creeps should be—" Cilla's eyes flashed, but she cut herself off. "I didn't come here to talk cop, I came to talk turkey."

"Oh?"

"As in Thanksgiving. Don't give me that look." Cilla angled her chin, readying for battle. "Every year you've got some excuse for not coming to Thanksgiving dinner, and this time I'm not buying it."

"Cilla, you know I appreciate the offer."

"The hell with that. You're family. We want you." Even as Althea was shaking her head, Cilla was plowing on. "Deb and Gage are coming. You haven't seen them in a year."

Althea thought of Cilla's younger sister, Deborah, and her husband. She would like to see Deb again. They'd gotten close while Deborah was in Denver finishing up college. And Gage Guthrie. Althea pursed her lips as she thought of him. She genuinely liked Deborah's husband, and a blind man could have seen that he adored his wife. But there was something about him—something Althea couldn't put her finger on. Not a bad thing, she thought now, not a worrying thing. But something.

"Taking a side trip?" Cilla asked.

"Sorry." Althea snapped back and fiddled with

the papers on her desk. "You know I'd love to see them again, Cilla, but—"

"They're bringing Adrianna." Cilla's secret weapon was her sister's baby girl, whom Althea had seen only in snapshots and videotapes. "You and I both know what a sucker you are for babies."

"You want to keep that down?" Althea stated with an uneasy glance toward the bull pen. "I've got a reputation to uphold around here." She sighed and leaned back in her chair. "You know I want to see them, all of them. And since I'm sure they'll be here through the holiday weekend, I will. We'll shoot for Saturday."

"Thanksgiving dinner." Cilla dusted her hands together as she straightened. "You're coming this year, if I have to tell Boyd to make it an order. I'm having my family. My whole family."

"Cilla—"

"That's it." Cilla folded her arms. "I'm taking this to the captain."

"You're in luck," Boyd said as he came to the door. "The captain happens to be available. And he's brought you a present." He stepped aside.

"Natalie!" With a whoop of pleasure, Cilla threw her arms around her sister-in-law and squeezed. "I thought you were in New York."

"I was." Natalie's dark green eyes sparkled with laughter as she drew Cilla back to kiss her. "I had to fly in for a few days, and I figured I'd make this my first stop. I didn't know I'd hit the jackpot. You look great."

"You look phenomenal, as always." It was perfectly true. The tall, willow-slim woman with the sleek blond hair and the conservatively cut suit would always turn heads. "The kids are going to be thrilled."

"I can't wait to get my hands on them." She turned, held out both hands. "Thea. I can't believe I'm lucky enough to get all three of you at once."

"It's really good to see you." With their hands still linked, Althea pressed her cheek to Natalie's. In the years Althea had been Boyd's partner, she and his younger sister had become fast friends. "How are your parents?"

"Terrific. They send love to everyone." In an old habit, she glanced around Althea's office, let out a sigh. "Thea, can't you at least get a space with a window?"

"I like this one. Fewer distractions."

"I'm calling Maria as soon as I get to the station," Cilla announced. "She'll whip up something special for tonight. You're coming, Thea."

"Wouldn't miss it."

"What is this?" Colt demanded as he tried to squeeze into the room. "A conference? Thea, you're going to have to get a bigger—" He broke off, stared. "Nat?"

Her stunned expression mirrored his. "Colt?"

His grin split his face. "Son of a gun." He elbowed past Boyd to grab Natalie in a hug that lifted her feet from the floor. "I'll be damned. Pretty Natalie. What's it been? Six years?"

"Seven." She kissed him full on the mouth. "We ran into each other in San Francisco."

"At the Giants game, right. You look better than ever."

"I am better than ever. Why don't we have a drink later, and catch up?"

"Now, that's…" He fumbled to a halt when he glanced at Althea. She was sitting on the edge of her desk, watching their reunion with an expression of mild curiosity and polite interest. When he realized his arm was still around Natalie's waist, he dropped it quickly to his side. "Actually, I, ah…"

How was a man supposed to talk to an old female friend when the woman he loved was studying him as if he were something smeared on a glass slide?

Natalie caught the look that passed between Althea and Colt. Surprise came first, then a chuckle she disguised by clearing her throat. Well, well, she thought, what an interesting stew she'd dropped into. She couldn't resist stirring the pot.

"Colt and I go way back," she said to Althea. "I had a terrible crush on him when I was a teenager." She smiled wickedly up at Colt. "I've been waiting for years for him to take advantage of it."

"Really?" Althea tapped a finger to her lips. "He doesn't strike me as being slow off the mark. A little dense, maybe, but not slow."

"You're right about that. Cute, too, isn't he?" She winked at Althea.

"In an overt sort of way," Althea agreed, enjoying Colt's discomfort. "Why don't you and I have that drink later, Natalie? It sounds as though you and I have quite a bit to chat about."

"It certainly does."

"I don't think this is the place to set up social engagements." Well aware that he was outnumbered and outgunned, Colt stuck his hands into his pockets. "Althea looks busy."

"Oh, I've got a minute or two. What are you doing in town, Natalie?"

"Business. Always nice when you can mix it

with pleasure. I have an emergency meeting in an hour with the board of directors on one of Boyd's and my downtown units. Owning real estate is a full-time job. Without proper management, it can be a huge headache," she explained.

"You don't happen to own one on Second Avenue, do you?" Althea asked.

"Mmm, no. Is one up for sale?" A gleam came into her eyes, and then she laughed. "It's a weakness," she explained. "There's something about owning property, even with all the problems that come with it."

"What's the trouble now?" Boyd asked, trying to work up some interest.

"The manager decided to up all the rents and keep the difference." Natalie said, her eyes hardening in startling contrast to her soft, lovely face. "I hate being duped."

"Pride," Boyd said, and tapped a finger on her nose. "You hate making a mistake."

"I didn't make a mistake." Her chin angled upward. "The man's résumé was outstanding." When Boyd continued to grin, she wrinkled her nose at him. "The problem is, you have to give a manager autonomy. You can't be everywhere at once. I remember one manager we had who was running a floating crap game in an empty apartment. He kept it rented under a fake name," she continued, nearly amused now. "He'd even filled out an application, complete with faked references. He made enough profit off the games to afford the overhead, so the rent came in like clockwork. I'd never have found out if someone hadn't tipped the cops and they raided the place. It turned out he'd done the same thing twice before."

"Good Lord," Althea said, looking stunned.

"Oh, it wasn't that bad," Natalie went on. "Actually, it was pretty exciting stuff. I just— What is it?" she demanded when Althea sprang to her feet.

"Let's move." Colt was already headed out the door.

Althea grabbed her coat and sprinted after him. "Boyd, run a make on—"

"Nieman," he called out. "I got it. You want backup?"

"I'll let you know."

When the room emptied, Natalie threw up her hands and stared at Cilla. "What brought that on?"

"Cops." Cilla shrugged. That said it all.

Chapter 12

"I can't believe we let that slip by us." Colt slammed the door to the Jeep and peeled away from the curb. This time he didn't bother to remove the parking ticket under the windshield wiper.

"We're going on a hunch," Althea reminded him. "We could very well get slapped down."

"You don't think so."

She shut her eyes a moment, letting the pieces fall into place. "It fits," she said grimly. "Not one single tenant could swear they'd ever seen this Mr. Davis. He was the man who wasn't there—maybe because he never was."

"And who would have had access to the penthouse? Who could have faked references—references that didn't have to exist? Who could have slipped through the building virtually unnoticed, because he was always there?"

"Nieman."

"I told you he was a weasel," Colt said between his teeth.

She was forced to agree, but cautiously. "Don't get ahead of yourself, Nightshade. We're doing some follow-up questioning. That's all."

"I'm getting answers," he shot back. "That's all."

"Don't make me pull rank on you, Colt." She said it quietly, calming him. "We're going in there to ask questions. We may be able to shake him into slipping up. We may very well have to walk out without him. But now we have a place to start digging."

They'd dig, all right, Colt thought. Deep enough to bury Nieman. "I'll follow your lead," he said. For now. He pulled up at a red light, drumming his fingers impatiently on the wheel. "I'd like to, ah...explain about Nat."

"Explain what?"

"That we aren't—weren't. Ever," he said savagely. "Got it?"

"Really?" She'd laugh about this later, she was

sure. Once there weren't so many other things on her mind. Still, she wasn't so preoccupied that she'd blow a chance to bait him. "Why not? She's beautiful, she's fun, she's smart. Looks like you fell down on that one, Nightshade."

"It wasn't that I didn't... I mean, I thought about it. Started to—" He swore, revved the engine when the light turned. "She was Boyd's sister, all right? Before I knew it, she was like my sister, too, so I couldn't...think about her that way."

She sent him a long, curious look. "Why are you apologizing?"

"I'm not." His voice took on a vicious edge, because he realized he was doing just that. "I'm explaining. Though God knows why I'd bother. You think what you want."

"All right. I think you're overreacting to a situation in typical, and predictable, male fashion." The look he speared at her should have sliced to the bone. She merely smiled. "I don't hold it against you. Any more than I would hold it against you if you and Natalie *had* been involved. The past is just that. I know that better than anyone."

"I guess you do." He jammed the gearshift into fourth, then reached out to cover her hand with his. "But we weren't involved."

"I'd have to say that was your loss, pal. She's terrific."

"So are you."

She smiled at him. "Yeah, I am."

Colt steered to the curb, parking carelessly in a loading zone. He waited while Althea called in their location. "Ready?"

"I'm always ready." She stepped out of the car. "I want to play this light," she told Colt. "Just follow-up questions. We've got nothing on him. Nothing. If we push too hard, we'll lose our chance. If we're right about this—"

"We are right. I can feel it."

So could she. She nodded. "Then I want him. For Liz. For Wild Bill." And for herself, she realized. To help her close the door this ordeal had opened again.

They walked in together and approached Nieman's apartment. Althea sent Colt one last warning look, then knocked.

"Yes, yes…" Nieman's voice came through the door. "What is it?"

"Lieutenant Grayson, Mr. Nieman." She held her shield up to the peephole. "Denver PD. We need a few minutes of your time."

He pulled open the door to the width of the security chain. His eyes darted from Althea's face to Colt's and back again. "Can't this wait? I'm busy."

"I'm afraid not. It shouldn't take long, Mr. Nieman. Just routine."

"Oh, very well." With a definite lack of grace, he yanked off the chain. "Come in, then."

When she did, Althea noted the packing boxes set on the carpet. Many were filled with shredded paper. For Althea, they were as damning as a smoking gun.

"As you can see, you've caught me at a bad time."

"Yes, I can see that. Are you moving, Mr. Nieman?"

"Do you think I would stay here, work here, after this—this scandal?" Obviously insulted, he tugged on his tightly knotted tie. "I think not. Police, reporters, badgering tenants. I haven't had a moment's peace since this began."

"I'm sure it's been a trial for you," Colt stated. He wanted to get his hands on that tie. Nieman would hang nicely from it.

"It certainly has. Well, I suppose you must sit." Nieman waved a hand toward chairs. "But I really can't spare much time. I've a great deal of packing left to do. I don't trust the movers to do it," he added. "Clumsy, always breaking things."

"You've had a lot of experience with moving?" This from Althea as she sat and took out her pad and pencil.

"Naturally. As I've explained before, I travel. I enjoy my work." He smiled by tightening his lips over his teeth. "But I find it tedious to remain in one place for too long. Landlords are always looking for a responsible, experienced manager."

"I'm sure they are." She tapped her pencil against the pad. "The owners of this building…" She began to flip pages.

"Johnston and Croy, Inc."

"Yes." She nodded when she found the notation. "They were quite upset when they were told about the activities in the penthouse."

"I should say." Nieman hitched up the knees of his trousers and sat. "They're a respectable company. Quite successful in the West and Southwest. Of course, they blame me. That's to be expected."

"Because you didn't do a personal interview with the tenant?" Althea prompted.

"The bottom line in real estate, Lieutenant, is regular monthly rentals and low turnover. I provided that."

"You also provided the scene of the crime."

"I can hardly be held responsible for the conduct of my tenants."

It was time, Althea decided, to take a risk. A calculated one. "And you never entered the premises? Never checked on it?"

"Why would I? I had no reason to bother Mr. Davis or go into the penthouse."

"You never went in while Mr. Davis was in residence?" Althea asked.

"I've just said I didn't."

She frowned, flipped more pages. "How would you explain your fingerprints?"

Something flickered in Nieman's eyes, then was gone. "I don't know what you mean."

She was reaching, but she pressed a bit further. "I wondered how you would explain it if I told you that your fingerprints were found inside the penthouse—since you claim never to have entered the premises."

"I don't see…" He was scrambling now. "Oh, yes, I remember now. A few days before…before the incident…the smoke alarm in the penthouse went off. Naturally, I used my passkey to investigate when no one answered my knock."

"You had a fire?" Colt asked.

"No, no, simply a defective smoke detector. It was so minor an incident, I quite forgot it."

"Perhaps you've forgotten something else," Althea said politely. "Perhaps you forgot to tell us about a cabin, west of Boulder. Do you manage that property, as well?"

"I don't know what you're talking about. I don't manage any property but this."

"Then you just use it for recreation," Althea continued. "With Mr. Donner, Mr. Kline and Mr. Scott."

"I have no knowledge of a cabin," Nieman said stiffly, but a line of sweat had popped out above his top lip. "Nor do I know any people by those names. Now you'll have to excuse me."

"Mr. Scott isn't quite up to visitors," Althea told him, and remained seated. "But we can go downtown and see Kline and Donner. That might refresh your memory."

"I'm not going anywhere with you." Nieman rose then. "I've answered all your questions in a reasonable and patient manner. If you persist in this harassment, I'll have to call my attorney."

"Feel free." Althea gestured toward the phone. "He can meet us at the station. In the meantime, I'd like you to think back to where you were on the night of October 25. You could use an alibi."

"Whatever for?"

"Murder."

"That's preposterous." He drew a handkerchief out of his breast pocket to wipe his face. "You can't come in here and accuse me this way."

"I'm not accusing you, Mr. Nieman. I'm asking for your whereabouts on October 25, between the hours of 9:00 and 11:00 p.m. You might also tell your lawyer that we'll be questioning you about a missing woman known as Lacy, and about the abduction of Elizabeth Cook, who is currently in protective custody. Liz is a very bright and observant girl, isn't she, Nightshade?"

"Yeah." She was amazing, Colt thought. Absolutely amazing. She was cracking Nieman into pieces with nothing but innuendo. "Between Liz and the sketches, the D.A. has plenty to work with."

"I don't believe we mentioned the sketches to Mr. Nieman." Althea closed her notebook. "Or the fact that both Kline and Donner were thoroughly interrogated yesterday. Of course, Scott is still critical, so we'll have to wait for his corroboration."

Nieman's face went pasty. "They're lying. I'm a respectable man. I have credentials." His voice cracked. "You can't prove anything on the word of some two-bit actors."

"I don't believe we mentioned Kline and Donner were actors, did we, Nightshade?"

"No." He could have kissed her. "No, we didn't."

"You must be psychic, Nieman," Althea stated. "Why don't we go to the station and see what else you can come up with?"

"I know my rights." Nieman's eyes glittered with rage as he felt the trap creaking shut. "I'm not going anywhere with you."

"I'll have to insist." Althea rose. "Go ahead and call your lawyer, Nieman, but you're coming in for questioning. Now."

"No woman's going to tell me what to do." Nieman lunged, and though Althea was braced, even eager, Colt stepped between them and merely used one hand to shove Nieman back onto the couch.

"Assaulting an officer," he said mildly. "I guess we'll take him in on that. It should give you enough time to get a search warrant."

"More than enough," she agreed. She took out her cuffs.

"Ah, Lieutenant…" Colt watched as she competently secured Nieman's skinny wrists. "They didn't find prints upstairs, did they?"

"I never said they did." She tossed her hair back. "I simply asked what he'd say *if* I said they were found."

"I was wrong," he decided. "I do like your style."

"Thanks." Satisfied, she smiled. "I wonder what we might find in all these neatly packed boxes."

They found more than enough. Tapes, snapshots, even a detailed journal in Nieman's own hand. It painstakingly recorded all his activities, all his thoughts, all his hatred for women. It described how the woman named Lacy had been murdered, and how her body had been buried behind the cabin.

By that afternoon, he had been booked on enough charges to keep him away from society for a lifetime.

"A little anticlimactic," Colt commented as he followed Althea into her office, where she would type up her report. "He was so revolting, I couldn't even drum up the energy to kill him."

"Lucky for you." She sat, booted up her machine. "Listen, if it's any consolation, I believe he was telling the truth about not touching Liz himself. I'm betting the psychiatric profile bears it out. Impotence, accompanied by rage against women and voyeuristic tendencies."

"Yeah, he just likes to watch." His fury came and went. Althea had been right about not being able to change what had been.

"And to make piles of money from his hobby," she added. "Once he rounded up his cameraman and a couple of sleazy actors, he went into the business of pandering to others with his peculiar tastes. Got to give him credit. He kept a very precise set of books on his porn business. Kept him in antiques and silk ties."

"He won't need either one in a cell." He rested his hands on her shoulders. "You did good, Thea. Real good."

"I usually do." She glanced over her shoulder to study him. Now all she had to do was figure out what to do about Colt. "Listen, Nightshade, I really want to get this paperwork moving, and then I need some downtime. Okay?"

"Sure. I hear there's going to be some spread at the Fletchers' tonight. Are you up for it?"

"You bet. Why don't I meet you there?"

"All right." He leaned down to press his lips to her hair. "I love you, Thea."

She waited until he left, shutting her door behind him. *I know,* she thought, *I love you, too.*

She went to see Liz. It helped to be able to give the girl and her family some sort of resolution. Colt had beaten her to it, had already come and gone. But Althea sensed that Liz needed to hear it from her, as well.

"We'll never be able to repay you." Marleen stood with her arm around Liz as if she couldn't bear not to touch her daughter. "I don't have the words to tell you how grateful we are."

"I—" She'd almost said she'd just been doing her job. It was the truth, but it wasn't all of it. "Just take care of each other," she said instead.

"We're going to spend a lot more time doing just that." Marleen pressed her cheek against Liz's. "We're going home tomorrow."

"We're going into family counseling," Liz told Althea. "And I—I'm going to join a rape victims' support group. I'm a little scared."

"It's all right to be scared."

Nodding, Liz looked at her mother. "Mom, can I—I just want to talk to Lieutenant Grayson for a minute."

"Sure." Marleen clung for a final moment. "I'll just go down to the lobby, help your father when he gets back with that ice cream."

"Thanks." Liz waited until her mother left the room. "Dad doesn't know how to talk about what happened to me yet. It's awful hard on him."

"He loves you. Give him time."

"He cried." Liz's own eyes filled with tears. "I never saw him cry before. I thought he was too busy with work and stuff to care. I was stupid to run away." Once she'd blurted it out, she exhaled deeply. "I didn't think they understood me, or what I wanted. Now I see how bad I hurt them. It won't ever be exactly the same again, will it?"

"No, Liz, it won't. But if you help each other through it, it can be better."

"I hope so. I still feel so empty inside. Like a part of me's not there anymore."

"You'll fill it with something else. You can't let this block off your feelings for other people. It can make you strong, Liz, but you don't want it to make you hard."

"Colt said—" She sniffled and reached for the box of tissues her mother had left on the coffee table. "He said whenever I felt like I couldn't make it, I should think of you."

Althea stared. "Of me?"

"Because you'd had something horrible happen to you, and you'd used it to make yourself beautiful. Inside and out. That you hadn't just survived, you'd triumphed." She gave a watery smile. "And I could, too. It was funny to hear him talk that way. I guess he must like you a lot."

"I like him, too." And she did, Althea realized. It wasn't a weakness to love someone, not when you could admire and respect him at the same time. Not when he saw exactly what you were, and loved you back.

"Colt's the best," Liz stated. "He never lets you down, you know? No matter what."

"I think I do."

"I was wondering… I know the counseling's important, and everything, but I wonder if I could just call you sometimes. When I—when I don't think I can get through it."

"I hope you will." Althea rose to go over and sit beside Liz. She opened her arms. "You call when you're feeling bad. And when you're feeling good. We all need somebody who understands us."

Fifteen minutes later, Althea left the Cooks to their ice cream and their privacy. She decided she had a lot of thinking to do. She'd always known where her life was going. Now that it had taken this sudden and dramatic detour, she needed to get her bearings again.

But Colt was waiting for her in the lobby.

"Hey, Lieutenant." He tipped her head back and kissed her lightly.

"What are you doing here? Marleen said you'd been by already."

"I went with Frank. He needed to talk."

She touched a hand to his cheek. "You're a good friend, Nightshade."

"It's the only kind of friend there is." She smiled, because she knew he meant it. "Want a lift?"

"I've got my car." But when they walked outside together, she discovered she didn't want that downtime alone after all. "Look, do you want to take a walk or something? I'm wired."

"Sure." He draped an arm casually over her shoulder. "You can help me scope out some of the shop windows. My mother has a birthday next week."

Resistance surged instantly—a knee-jerk response. "I'm no good at picking out presents for people I don't know."

"You'll get to know her." He strolled to the corner and turned left, heading toward a row of downtown shops. He glanced in one window at an elegant display of fine china and crystal. "Hey, you're not the type who, like, registers a pattern and that stuff, are you? You know, for wedding presents?"

"Get a grip." She moved past him so that he had to lengthen his stride to catch up.

"What about a trousseau? Do women still do that?"

"I haven't any idea, or any interest."

"It's not that I mind the T-shirt you wore in bed last night. I was just thinking that something a little more…no, a little less, would be nice for the honeymoon. Where do you want to go?"

"Are you going to cut this out?"

"No."

With an impatient breath, she turned and stared at the next window. "That's a nice sweater." She pointed to a rich blue cowl-neck on a mannequin. "Maybe she'd go for cashmere."

"Maybe." He nodded. "Fine. Let's go get it."

"See, that's your problem." Althea whirled around, hands on hips. "You don't give anything enough thought. You look at one thing, and boom—that's it."

"When it's the right thing, why look around?" He smiled and tugged on her hair. "I know what works for me when I see it. Come on." He took her hand and pulled her into the shop. "The blue sweater in the window?" he said to the clerk. "Have you got it in a size…" He measured in the air with his hands.

"Ten?" the clerk guessed. "Certainly, sir. Just one moment."

"You didn't ask how much it cost," Althea pointed out.

"When something's right, cost is irrelevant." He turned to smile at her. "You're going to keep me in line. I appreciate that. I tend to let details slip."

"There's news." She stepped away to poke through a rack of silk blouses.

He was careless, Althea reminded herself. He was impulsive and rash and quick on the draw. All the things she was not. She preferred order, routine, meticulous calculation. She had to be crazy to think they could mesh.

She turned her head, watching him as he waited for the clerk to ring up the sweater and gift-wrap it.

But they did mesh, she realized. Everything about him fitted her like a glove. The hair wasn't really blond or brown and was never quite disciplined. The eyes, caught somewhere between blue and green, that could stop her heart with one look. His recklessness. His dependability.

His total and unconditional understanding.

"Problem?" he asked when he caught her staring.

"No."

"Would you like a pink bow, sir, or blue?"

"Pink," he said, without glancing back. "Do you have any wedding dresses in here?"

"Not formal ones, no, sir." But the clerk's eyes lit up at the prospect of another sale. "We do have some very elegant tea gowns and cocktail suits that would be perfect for a wedding."

"It should be something festive," he decided, and the humor was back in his eyes. "For New Year's Eve."

Althea straightened her shoulders, turned on her heel to face him. "Get this, Nightshade. I am not marrying you on New Year's Eve."

"Okay, okay. Pick another date."

"Thanksgiving," she told him, and had the pleasure of watching his mouth fall open as he dropped the box the clerk had handed him.

"What?"

"I said Thanksgiving. Take it or leave it." She tossed her hair back and strode out the door.

"Wait! Damn!" He started after her, kicked the gift box halfway across the room. The clerk called after him as he scooped it up on the run.

"Sir, the dresses?"

"Later." He swung through the door and caught up with Althea halfway down the block. "Did you say you'd marry me on Thanksgiving?"

"I hate repeating myself, Nightshade. If you can't keep up, that's your problem. Now, if you've finished your shopping, I'm going back to work."

"Just one damn minute." Exasperated, he stuffed the box under his arm, crushing the bow. It freed his hands to snag her by the shoulders. "What made you change your mind?"

"It must have been your smooth, subtle approach," she said dryly. Lord, she was enjoying this, she realized. Deep-down enjoying it. "Keep manhandling me, pal, and I'll haul you in."

He shook his head, as if to realign his thoughts. "You're going to marry me?"

She arched a brow. "Ain't no flies on you."

"On Thanksgiving. *This* Thanksgiving. The one that's coming up in a few weeks?"

"Getting cold feet already?" she began, then found her mouth much too occupied for words. It was a heady kiss, filled with promises and joy. "Do you know the penalty for kissing a police officer on a public street?" she asked when she could speak again.

"I'll risk it."

"Good." She dragged his mouth back to hers. Pedestrians wound around them as they clung. "You're going to get life for this, Nightshade."

"I'm counting on it." Carefully he drew her back so that he could see her face. "Why Thanksgiving?"

"Because I'd like to have a family to celebrate it with. Cilla's always bugging me to join them, but I...I couldn't."

"Why?"

"Is this an interrogation or an engagement?" she demanded.

"Both, but this is the last one. Why are you going to marry me?"

"Because you nagged me until I broke down. And I felt sorry for you, because you seemed so set on it. Besides, I love you, and I've kind of gotten used to you, so—"

"Hold on. Say that again."

"I said I've kind of gotten used to you."

Grinning, he kissed the tip of her nose. "Not that part. The part right before that."

"Where I felt sorry for you?"

"Uh-uh. After that."

"Oh, the I-love-you part."

"That's the one. Say it again."

"Okay." She took a deep breath. "I love you." And let it out. "It's tougher to say it all by itself that way."

"You'll get used to it."

"I think you're right."

He laughed and crushed her against him. "I'm betting on it."

Epilogue

"I think I need to consider this again."

Althea stood in front of the full-length mirror in Cilla's bedroom, staring at her own reflection. There was a woman inside the mirror, she noted dispassionately. A pale woman with a tumble of red hair. She looked elegant in a slim ivory suit trimmed with lace and accented with tiny pearl buttons that ran the length of the snugly fitted jacket.

But her eyes were too big, too wide, and too fearful.

"I really don't think this is going to work."

"You look fabulous," Deborah assured her. "Perfect."

"I wasn't talking about the dress." She pressed a hand to her queasy stomach. "I meant the wedding."

"Don't start." Cilla tugged at the line of Althea's ivory silk jacket. "You're fidgeting again."

"Of course I'm fidgeting." For lack of anything better to do, Althea reached up to make sure the pearl drops at her ears were secure. Colt's mother had given them to her, she remembered, and felt a trickle of warmth at the memory. Something to be handed down, his mother had said, as they had been from Colt's grandmother to her.

Then she'd cried a little, and kissed Althea's cheek and welcomed her to the family.

Family, Althea thought on a fresh wave of panic. What did she know about family?

"I'm about to commit myself for life to a man I've known a matter of weeks," she muttered to the woman in the mirror. "I should *be* committed."

"You love him, don't you?" Deborah asked.

"What does that have to do with it?"

Laughing, Deborah took Althea's restless hand in hers. "Only everything. I didn't know Gage very long, either." And had known the depths of his secrets for an even shorter time. "But I loved him, and I knew. I've seen the way you look at Colt, Thea. You know, too."

"Lawyers," Althea complained to Cilla. "They always turn things around on you."

"She's great, isn't she?" Pride burst through as Cilla gave her sister a hard squeeze. "The best prosecutor east of the Mississippi."

"When you're right, you're right," Deborah returned with a grin. "Now, let's take a look at the matron of honor." She tilted her head to examine her sister. "You look wonderful, Cilla."

"So do you." Cilla brushed a hand through her sister's dark hair. "Marriage and motherhood agree with you."

"If you two will finish up your admiration hour, I'm having a nervous breakdown over here." Althea sat down on the bed, squeezed her eyes shut. "I could make a run for it out the back."

"He'd catch you," Cilla decided.

"Not if I had a really good head start. Maybe if I—" A knock on the door interrupted her. "If that's Nightshade, I am not going to talk to him."

"Of course not," Deborah agreed. "Bad luck." She opened the door to her husband and daughter. That was good luck, she thought as she smiled at Gage. The very best luck of all.

"Sorry to break in on the prep work, but we've got some restless people downstairs."

"If those kids have touched that wedding cake…" Cilla began.

"Boyd saved it," Gage assured her. Barely. With the baby tucked in one arm, he slipped the other around his wife. "Colt's wearing a path in the den carpet."

"So he's nervous," Althea shot back. "He should be. Look what he's gotten us into. Boy, would I like to be a fly on the wall down there."

Gage grinned, winked at Deborah. "It has its advantages." He nuzzled his infant daughter when she began to fuss.

"I'll take her, Gage." Deborah gathered Adrianna into her arms. "You go help Boyd calm down the groom. We're nearly ready."

"Who said?" Althea twisted her hands together.

Cilla brushed Gage out of the room, closed the door. It was time for the big guns. "Coward," she said softly.

"Now, just a minute…"

"You're afraid to walk downstairs and make a public commitment to the man you love. That's pathetic."

Catching on, Deborah soothed the baby, and

played the game. "Now, Cilla, don't be so harsh. If she's changed her mind—"

"She hasn't. She just can't make it up. And Colt's doing everything to make her happy. He's selling his ranch, buying land out here."

Althea got to her feet. "That's unfair."

"It certainly is." Deborah ranged herself beside Althea, and bit the inside of her lip to keep from grinning. "I'd think you'd be a little more understanding, Cilla. This is an important decision."

"Then she should make it instead of hiding up here like some vestal virgin about to be sacrificed."

Althea's chin jutted out. "I'm not hiding. Deb, go out and tell them to start the damn music. I'm coming down."

"All right, Thea. If you're sure." Deborah patted her arm, winked at her sister, and hurried out.

"Well, come on." Althea stormed to the door. "Let's get going."

"Fine." Cilla sauntered past her, then started down the steps.

Althea was nearly to the bottom before she realized she'd been conned. The two sisters had pulled off the good cop–bad cop routine like pros.

Now her stomach jumped. There were flowers everywhere, banks of color and scent. There was

music, soft, romantic. She saw Colt's mother leaning heavily against his father and smiling bravely
through a mist of tears. She saw Natalie beaming
and dabbing at her eyes. Deborah, her lashes wet,
cradling Adrianna.

There was Boyd, reaching out to take Cilla's
hand, kissing her damp cheek before looking back
at Althea to give her an encouraging wink.

Althea came to a dead stop. If people cried at
weddings, she deduced, there had to be a good reason.

Then she looked toward the fireplace, and saw
nothing but Colt.

And he saw nothing but her.

Her legs stopped wobbling. She crossed to him,
carrying a single white rose, and her heart.

"Good to see you, Lieutenant," he murmured as
he took her hand.

"Good to see you, too, Nightshade." She felt
the warmth from the fire that glowed beside
them, the warmth from him. She smiled as he
brought her hand to his lips, and her fingers were
steady.

"Happy Thanksgiving."

"Same goes." She brought their joined hands to
her lips in turn. Maybe she didn't know about fam-

ily, but she'd learn. They'd learn. "I love you, very much."

"Same goes. Ready for this?"

"I am now."

As the fire crackled, they faced each other and the life they'd make together.

* * * * *

Danger walks in the darkness…

Don't miss the next instalment of

NIGHT TALES.

Night Smoke
by
Nora Roberts

"Midnight. Witching hour. Wait and see."

A fire at Natalie Fletcher's south side warehouse is an inconvenient accident – isn't it? As far as she knows, she has no enemies, no one who would want to destroy her fledgling business. Then an investigation discovers arson, and Natalie begins to worry.

When Natalie's office is set ablaze, she's horrified. But it's the mysterious phone call that warned of a midnight attack which convinces her that this is personal. And as each fire is set, lives are endangered. Natalie has to find out who wants her ruined – before someone is killed…

Read on for a preview!

NIGHT SMOKE

Fire. It cleansed. It destroyed. With its heat, lives could be saved. Or lives could be taken. It was one of the greatest discoveries of man, and one of his chief fears.

And one of his fascinations.

Mothers warned their children not to play with matches, not to touch the red glow of the stove. For no matter how pretty the flame, how seductive the warmth, fire against flesh burned.

In the hearth, it was romantic, cozy, cheerful, dancing and crackling, wafting scented smoke and flickering soft golden light. Old men dreamed by it. Lovers wooed by it.

In the campfire, it shot its sparks toward a starry sky, tempting wide-eyed children to roast their marshmallows into black goo while shivering over ghost stories.

There were dark, hopeless corners of the city where the homeless cupped their frozen hands over trash-can fires, their faces drawn and weary in the shadowy light, their minds too numb for dreams.

In the city of Urbana, there were many fires.

A carelessly dropped cigarette smoldering in a mattress. Faulty wiring, overlooked, or ignored by a corrupt inspector. A kerosene heater set too close to the drapes, oily rags tossed in a stuffy closet. A flash of lightning. An unattended candle. All could cause destruction of property, loss of life. Ignorance, an accident, an act of God.

But there were other ways, more devious ways.

Once inside the building he took several short, shallow breaths. It was so simple, really. And so exciting. The power was in his hands now. He knew exactly what to do, and there was a thrill in doing it. Alone. In the dark.

It wouldn't be dark for long. The thought made him giggle as he climbed to the second floor. He would soon make the light.

Two cans of gasoline would be enough. With the first he splashed the old wooden floor, soaking it, leaving a trail as he moved from wall to wall, from room to room. Now and again he stopped, pulling stock from the racks, scattering matchbooks over the stream of flammables, adding fuel that would feed the flames and spread them.

The smell of the accelerant was sweet, an exotic perfume that heightened his senses. He wasn't panicked, he wasn't hurried as he climbed the winding metal stairs to the next floor. He was quiet, of course, for he wasn't a stupid man. But he knew the night watchman was bent over his magazines in another part of the building.

As he worked, he glanced up at the spider-like sprinklers in the ceiling. He'd already seen to those. There would be no hiss of water from the pipes as the flames rose, no warning buzz from smoke alarms.

This fire would burn, and burn, and burn, until the window glass exploded from the angry fists of heat. Paint would blister, metal would melt, rafters would fall, charred and flaming.

He wished...for a moment he wished he could stay, stand in the center of it all and watch the sleeping fire awaken, grumbling. He wanted to be there, to admire and absorb as it stirred, snapped, then stretched its hot, bright body. He wanted to hear its triumphant roar as it hungrily devoured everything in its path.

But he would be far away by then. Too far to see, to hear, to smell. He would have to imagine it.

With a sigh, he lit the first match, held the flame at eye level, admiring the infant spark, mesmerized by it. He was smiling, as proud as any expectant father, as he tossed the tiny fire into a dark pool of gas. He watched for a moment, only a moment, as the animal erupted into life, streaking along the trail he'd left for it.

He left quietly, hurrying now, into the frigid night. Soon his feet had picked up the rhythm of his racing heart.

© Nora Roberts 1994

Passion. Power. Suspense.
It's time to fall under the spell of Nora Roberts.

From No. 1 *New York Times* bestselling author Nora Roberts

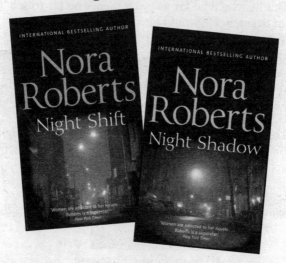

Night Shift

When her stalker's threats start to escalate, late-night DJ Cilla O'Roarke and Detective Boyd Fletcher are led into a terrifying situation that they might not both walk away from...

Night Shadow

Faced with a choice between her own life and the law, can prosecutor Deborah O'Roarke make the right decision – before someone else dies?

From No. 1 *New York Times* bestselling author Nora Roberts

Nightshade
When a teenager gets caught up in making sadistic violent films, Colt Nightshade and Lieutenant Althea Grayson must find her before she winds up dead...

Night Smoke
When Natalie Fletcher's office is set ablaze, she must find out who wants her ruined – before someone is killed...

Night Shield
When a revengeful robber leaves blood-stained words on Detective Allison Fletcher's walls, she knows her cop's shield won't be enough to protect her...

**Passion. Power. Suspense.
It's time to fall under the spell of Nora Roberts.**

The Donovan Legacy

Four cousins. Four stories. One terrifying secret.

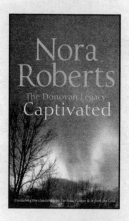
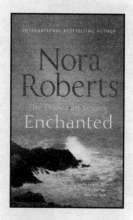
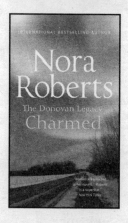
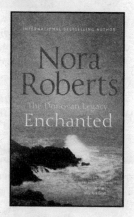